WHISPERS OF THE KAMI

Delving into the Mystical Realms of Japanese Mythology: Gods, Spirits, and Legends

Aria Nakamura

Summary

CHAPTER 1: INTRODUCTION TO THE DIVINE DANCE

Japanese mythology is an intricate tapestry of gods, creatures, and tales that mirror the country's rich cultural heritage and the delicate balance of nature. At the heart of these tales is a dance—a dance of creation, destruction, renewal, and balance. This divine dance weaves together themes of love, conflict, sacrifice, and redemption.

The islands of Japan, surrounded by deep oceans and crowned by majestic mountains, have birthed legends that capture the imagination and offer insights into the human condition. From the story of Izanagi and Izanami, the primordial couple who gave birth to the islands, to Amaterasu, the radiant sun goddess who hid in a cave, casting the world into darkness, these myths do more than just entertain. They elucidate the complex interplay between man, nature, and the divine.

One cannot delve into Japanese mythology without recognizing its roots in Shinto beliefs. Shintoism, the indigenous religion of Japan, places a heavy emphasis on kami—the spirits or deities associated with natural phenomena. Every mountain, river, and rock might house a kami, making nature itself a living, sacred entity. The dance of these deities reflects the rhythms of nature, from the cherry blossoms' fleeting beauty to the relentless force of the sea.

The dance in Japanese mythology is also evident in the various festivals or matsuri celebrated throughout the country. These festivals, with their rituals, music, and dances, often reenact mythological stories, bringing them to life in the modern world and ensuring that they are passed down to future generations.

This exploration into the divine dance of Japanese mythology will take readers on a journey through time, delving into ancient tales and understanding their continued relevance today. We'll waltz with the deities, tango with the tantalizing spirits, and sway with the stories that have shaped the Japanese psyche for millennia.

So, lace up your dancing shoes and prepare to be swept off your feet by the mesmerizing moves of Japan's most famous myths.

The Heartbeat of Japan: Mythology's Role

Japan, an archipelago off the eastern coast of Asia, has a rich and vibrant history that spans thousands of years. From its ancient traditions to its modern technological advancements, Japan has always been a land that balances the old and the new. At the core of Japanese culture lies a diverse and captivating mythology, which has had a profound influence on the society, art, and collective imagination of the Japanese people. In this chapter, we will delve into the heartbeat of Japan, exploring the multifaceted role of mythology in shaping the cultural and spiritual landscape of this remarkable country.

Origins: Creation Myths and the Japanese Pantheon

Every culture has its creation myths, and Japan is no exception. Japanese mythology often refers to the Kojiki ("Records of Ancient Matters") and the Nihon Shoki ("The Chronicles of Japan"), two ancient texts that chronicle the early history of Japan and its mythological origins. These texts provide us with a glimpse into a world where gods and goddesses, known as kami, play a pivotal role in the creation and governance of the universe.

One prominent creation myth in Japanese mythology is the story of Izanagi and Izanami, a divine couple who are believed to have birthed the Japanese islands and numerous deities. According to legend, Izanagi and Izanami stood on the Floating Bridge of Heaven and stirred the primordial sea with a jeweled spear. As they lifted the spear, the droplets that fell turned into islands, forming what we now recognize as Japan. This creation myth not only provides a poetic explanation for the unique geography of Japan but also establishes a foundation for the belief that the natural world and the divine are inherently connected.

The Japanese pantheon comprises an intricate network of deities, each with their own distinct role and influence. Some of the most well-known gods and goddesses in Japanese mythology include Amaterasu, the Sun Goddess; Susanoo, the God of Storms; and Tsukuyomi, the Moon God. These deities, along with countless others, have shaped the Japanese imagination and continue to be revered in both religious and popular culture contexts to this day.

Shinto: The Way of the Kami

At the heart of Japanese mythology lies Shinto, the national religion of Japan. Shinto, which translates to "the way of the kami," is a complex belief system that intertwines mythology, ritual practices, and reverence for nature. Unlike many other religions, Shinto does not have a single founder, nor does it adhere to a strict set of dogmas. Instead, it centers around the veneration of kami, which can be understood as divine, nature-based spirits.

Shinto is deeply embedded within Japanese society, with its practices and traditions permeating daily life. From visiting Shinto shrines to participating in religious festivals, the Japanese people maintain a close connection with their mythological heritage, seeking blessings and guidance from the kami. Shinto's emphasis on harmony with nature has also informed Japanese traditions such as gardening, tea ceremonies, and even the art of bonsai, showcasing the profound influence of mythology on various aspects of Japanese culture.

Folklore and Legends: Tales from the Past

In addition to the deities of Japanese mythology, folklore and legends play an integral role in shaping the cultural fabric of Japan. These stories, often passed down through generations, have served as a means of entertainment, moral instruction, and cultural preservation. Folklore, in contrast to the hereditary nature of mythology, encompasses a wide range of narratives involving supernatural creatures, ghosts, and heroes.

One well-known character from Japanese folklore is Momotaro, the Peach Boy. Born from a giant peach found floating down a river, Momotaro grows up to become a brave warrior. He embarks on a perilous journey to defeat an island of demons, ultimately showcasing the triumph of good over evil. The story of Momotaro, like many others in Japanese folklore, embodies important cultural values such as bravery, loyalty, and the power of teamwork.

Folklore also introduces mythical creatures, such as the Kitsune (the fox) and the Tengu (the bird-like creature), which have become staples of Japanese tales. These creatures often possess extraordinary powers, shape-shifting abilities, and an intricate interplay between good and evil, blurring the lines between the human and the supernatural realms. Such narratives not only entertain but also provide insights into the collective psyche of the Japanese people, reflecting their beliefs, fears, and aspirations.

Art and Literature: Mythological Inspirations

The significance of mythology in Japanese culture can be observed not only in its religious and folkloric aspects but also in its artistic expressions. Japanese art and literature have drawn heavily from mythological themes, nurturing a distinctive aesthetic that captures the essence of the supernatural and the divine.

In traditional Japanese art, representations of mythical creatures, gods, and goddesses abound. From ukiyo-e woodblock prints to vibrant paintings on folding screens, these artworks transport viewers into mythological realms where humans interact with the divine. Iconic figures like the Dragon God Ryu, the Goddess of Mercy Kannon, and the deities from the Twelve Heavenly Generals continue to inspire contemporary artists, imbuing their creations with a sense of awe and spirituality.

Japanese literature, too, has been deeply influenced by mythology. Classic works such as "The Tale of Genji" by Murasaki Shikibu and the poetry collection "Manyoshu" frequently reference mythological figures and share themes that resonate with mythological narratives, including love, honor, and the human condition. These literary masterpieces have had a lasting impact on Japanese storytelling, influencing modern novels, manga, and anime, ensuring that the mythological heartbeat of Japan continues to resonate with each new generation.

In this chapter, we have explored the intricate role of mythology in shaping the cultural and spiritual landscape of Japan. From creation myths and the Japanese pantheon to Shinto beliefs and folklore, the heartbeat of Japan can be felt in the rich tapestry woven by centuries of diverse mythological narratives. Moreover, mythology has not only laid the foundation for religious practices but has also left an indelible mark on traditional and contemporary art forms.

As we delve deeper into the fascinating world of Japanese mythology, we will uncover more tales, gods, and legends that continue to inspire and captivate. In subsequent chapters, we will explore specific mythological themes, iconic deities, and the enduring legacy of mythology in Japan's vibrant society. Together, we will embark on a journey that unveils the magic, wisdom, and interconnectedness of a mythology that beats at the heart of Japan.

Kami: The Ever-Present Spirits of Nature

The wind howled through the dense forest, carrying with it an eerie yet tranquil energy. The leaves rustled in unison, as if in conversation with invisible beings that inhabited the vast realm of nature. These beings, known as kami, were the ever-present spirits that dwelled within every corner of the natural world, abiding by a sacred code that governed the balance and harmony of existence.

Deep within the heart of Japan, a land known for its enchanted landscapes and captivating folklore, the concept of kami had been woven into the fabric of society for centuries. From majestic mountains to bubbling rivers, and from towering trees to delicate flowers, kami were believed to reside in every natural element, governing their essence and bestowing blessings upon those who revered them.

The identity of kami was both elusive and diverse, defying simple definition. They took on various forms, encompassing ancient gods, deified ancestors, and even divine essences embodied in rocks and waterfalls. These spirits were not bound by the limitations of human perception, but rather existed beyond the realm of comprehension. Though unseen, their presence could be felt in every breath of fresh air, every sunbeam that caressed the skin, and every gentle whisper that swayed the grass.

The interplay between humans and kami was a delicate dance, a relationship rooted in reverence and respect. The indigenous people of Japan, guided by a deep sense of spirituality, understood that the world inhabited by kami was entwined with their own. They knew that by coexisting in harmony with these spirits, they would be granted protection, guidance, and a vital connection to the natural order of things.

In the sacred groves dotting the countryside, Shinto priests would offer prayers and perform rituals to honor the kami. These rituals originated from a belief that the natural environment was sacred and imbued with divine presence. By paying homage to the spirits, people sought to appease and maintain a sense of balance within the delicate ecosystem.

One of the most revered kami in Japanese folklore was Amaterasu, the goddess of the sun. She was believed to be the ancestor of the imperial family and the bringer of light and life to the world. It was said that her radiance painted the sky with vibrant colors at dawn, evoking a sense of awe and gratitude from all who witnessed it. Every morning, villagers would greet the rising sun, acknowledging Amaterasu's power and offering thanks for the blessings bestowed upon them.

Another kami, Susano-O, the god of the sea and storms, personified the forces of nature in their most ferocious and unpredictable state. Susano-O's tempestuous nature was both feared and revered, as his anger could unleash devastating storms upon the lands. Sailors and fishermen danced a delicate balancing act, seeking the god's favor to ensure safe journeys on treacherous waters.

Nature itself, in its raw beauty, was considered a manifestation of the kami. The towering Mount Fuji, with its snow-capped peak piercing the heavens, was believed to be the dwelling place of a powerful kami. Biologists and geologists may have described it as a stratovolcano, but to the people of Japan, it was a sacred entity to be admired and worshipped.

As the seasons changed, so did the manifestations of the kami. The cherry blossoms, delicately adorning the landscape each spring, were looked upon as the kami of flowers. Their ephemeral beauty served as a reminder of the transient nature of life, urging all to appreciate and cherish the present moment. Festivals celebrating the bloom of cherry blossoms became moments of reflection and introspection, as people embraced the wisdom of the kami and pondered the fleeting nature of existence.

The belief in kami extended beyond the natural world, encompassing everyday objects and activities. Rice, the staple food of Japan, was seen as a sacred gift from the kami, a life-sustaining force ensuring the well-being of the people. Before planting the precious seed, farmers would offer prayers and rituals to the kami of the rice fields, expressing gratitude for the abundance they would receive.

The practice of tea ceremonies also held deep spiritual significance, as participants sought to create a sacred space in which the kami could be honored. The motions of pouring and sipping tea were conducted with utmost care and reverence, fostering a sense of tranquility and mindfulness. In these moments, the kami were invited to partake in the ritual, infusing it with their divine presence.

The profound respect for nature and the spirits it held resonated beyond the shores of Japan. In recent decades, the concept of kami has captivated the hearts of people around the world, offering a perspective that transcends cultural boundaries. As humanity grapples with the consequences of environmental exploitation and climate change, the belief in kami serves as a guiding light, reminding us of the interconnectedness between our actions and the natural world.

Through the eyes of the kami, humans are the stewards of the Earth, entrusted with the responsibility to protect and care for the delicate balance of nature. Just as the indigenous people of Japan understood, we too must strive to live in harmony with the spirits of our environment, recognizing that the preservation of the natural world is the preservation of our own existence.

So, let the wind carry the whispers of the kami, guiding us towards a world where reverence for nature is not just a remnant of ancient folklore but a guiding principle of our lives. Let us learn from the spirits that dwell within the rustling leaves and babbling brooks, and together, let us forge a future where the lessons of the kami resonate in every step we take.

Storytelling: Japan's Timeless Medium

In the land of the rising sun, storytelling has been an integral part of Japanese culture since ancient times. From the epic tales of warriors and heroes to the delicate art of haiku, Japan has nurtured a rich tradition of storytelling that has captivated audiences for centuries. In this chapter, we will delve into the multifaceted nature of storytelling in Japan, exploring its historical roots, its various forms, and its enduring legacy in contemporary society.

1. The Origins of Japanese Storytelling:

The origins of Japanese storytelling can be traced back to the early centuries of the Common Era when oral traditions were the primary means of communication. At this time, storytellers known as "rhapsodists" would travel from village to village, regaling audiences with tales of gods, demons, and mythical creatures. These rhapsodists were the custodians of Japan's ancient folklore, passing down stories from one generation to the next.

One such form of storytelling that emerged during this era was the art of Kamishibai, which literally translates to "paper theater." Kamishibai involved the use of illustrated cards placed inside a wooden frame as a visual aid to accompany the storyteller's narrative. This early form of storytelling laid the groundwork for later developments in Japanese storytelling.

2. The Rise of Written Literature:

With the introduction of writing to Japan in the 5th century, storytelling took on a new dimension. The advent of kana, a phonetic writing system, allowed greater accessibility to literature, leading to the emergence of written storytelling.

One of the most significant works of Japanese literature, "The Tale of Genji" by Lady Murasaki Shikibu, exemplifies the power of storytelling during this period. Written in the 11th century, it recounts the amorous adventures of Genji, a nobleman, and has since become a timeless masterpiece that continues to captivate readers worldwide. Lady Murasaki's work paved the way for future generations of Japanese authors, establishing a literary tradition that endures to this day.

3. Traditional Forms of Storytelling:

(a) Noh Theater:

Noh theater, a form of classical Japanese theater, combines music, dance, and storytelling to create a captivating performance. Developed in the 14th century, Noh plays often incorporate themes from mythology and folklore, with actors donning elaborate masks and costumes. Employing slow, deliberate movements and a unique vocal style, Noh storytelling transports audiences to a spectral realm, where spirits and mortals interact in surrealistic dramas.

(b) Rakugo:

Rakugo, a form of comedic storytelling, emerged during the Edo period (1603-1868). In Rakugo performances, a lone performer, known as a rakugoka, sits on a minimalistic stage, armed only with a fan and a small cloth as props. The rakugoka uses witty dialogue and exaggerated gestures to narrate humorous stories, often involving clever twists and wordplay. Rakugo serves as a quintessential example of the power of spoken storytelling, relying solely on the performer's vocal talents and physicality to engage the audience.

(c) Kabuki Theater:

Kabuki is a vibrant and colorful form of theater that originated in the early 17th century. With its extravagant costumes, makeup, and dramatic plotlines, Kabuki showcases the storytelling through its actors' physical performances. Combining elements of dance, song, and dialogue, Kabuki delights audiences with its larger-than-life characters and visually stunning stagecraft.

4. Storytelling in Contemporary Japan:

As Japan modernized and embraced new forms of entertainment, storytelling remained a vital part of its cultural fabric. While traditional storytelling forms continue to thrive, contemporary Japan has also embraced new mediums to convey stories.

(a) Manga:

Manga, Japanese comic books, have gained immense popularity both in Japan and worldwide. With their expressive artwork and engrossing narratives, manga captivates readers of all ages. From the epic adventures of "Dragon Ball" to the introspective coming-of-age stories of "Marmalade Boy," manga has become an integral part of Japan's modern storytelling landscape.

(b) Anime:

Anime, Japanese animated series and films, has also become a global phenomenon, attracting audiences with its visually stunning animation and compelling storylines. Iconic anime such as "Spirited Away" and "Naruto" have garnered international acclaim, demonstrating the enduring power of Japanese storytelling in the modern age.

(c) Video Games:

Japan's vibrant gaming industry also serves as a medium for storytelling. With narrative-driven games such as "Final Fantasy" and "The Legend of Zelda," players immerse themselves in rich, interactive worlds brought to life by engaging storytelling. The marriage of storytelling and technology has propelled Japanese video games to the forefront of the global gaming industry.

Storytelling in Japan has evolved and adapted throughout history, yet its essence remains unchanged. Whether told through ancient oral traditions, written literature, traditional theater, or modern mediums like manga, anime, and video games, storytelling continues to be a powerful and timeless medium in Japanese culture.

As we traverse the intricate tapestry of Japan's storytelling heritage, we discover a diverse range of narratives that transcend time, bridging the gaps between generations and cultures. The legacy of Japan's storytelling traditions lives on, ensuring its timeless appeal in an ever-changing world.

The Spiritual Landscape: From Sacred Mountains to Divine Waters

Japanese mythology is a rich tapestry of ancient beliefs, folklore, and legends that have shaped the spiritual landscape of the country. These myths not only provide insights into the cosmology and origins of Japan but also reflect the profound connection between nature and spirituality in Japanese culture. In this chapter, we will explore how sacred mountains and divine waters are central themes in Japanese mythology, serving as gateways to the spiritual realm and symbols of divinity.

The Sacred Mountains:

In Japanese mythology, mountains hold a special significance as places where gods and spirits of nature reside. Mount Fuji, Japan's most iconic peak, has been revered for centuries as a sacred site. According to ancient beliefs, Fuji was a dwelling place of various deities, serving as a bridge between the mortal and spiritual worlds. It is believed that by climbing Mount Fuji, one could cleanse their soul and achieve spiritual enlightenment.

Another famous sacred mountain is Mount Hiei, located near Kyoto. On its slopes lies the Enryaku-ji Temple, one of the most important Buddhist monasteries in Japan. The monks of Enryaku-ji dedicated themselves to ascetic practices and spiritual enlightenment. Mount Hiei, with its lush forests and meditative atmosphere, became a sanctuary for spiritual seekers and a place of pilgrimage.

Spiritual journeys to these sacred mountains were not limited to devout monks. Throughout history, emperors, aristocrats, and commoners alike sought solace and enlightenment in the presence of divine nature. These pilgrimages not only served as a means of connecting with the gods but also showcased the resilience and determination of the Japanese people to explore the sacred within themselves.

Divine Waters:

Water is another element deeply intertwined with the spiritual landscape of Japan. The archipelago is blessed with countless rivers, lakes, waterfalls, and hot springs that are considered sacred. These bodies of water are believed to be inhabited by water deities, guardians of purity and fertility.

One such legendary location is the Nachi Falls in Wakayama Prefecture. With its impressive 133-meter drop, it is regarded as one of Japan's most beautiful waterfalls. According to folklore, a deity named Nachi-no-Otaki resides within the falls, overseeing the spiritual well-being of the region. Many pilgrims visit the site to pay their respects and seek the divine blessings of the deity.

Hot springs, or onsen, also hold great spiritual significance in Japanese mythology. These naturally occurring thermal baths are believed to possess healing properties for both the body and soul. The most famous onsen is located in the small town of Dogo in Ehime Prefecture. The Dogo Onsen, with its elaborate wooden architecture, has been a sanctuary for rest and rejuvenation for over a thousand years. It is said to have been frequented by gods and spirits, making it a place of great spiritual power.

Sacred Waters and Rituals:

Water in Japanese mythology is not only revered for its symbolism but also for its use in various purification rituals. Before entering shrines or temples, it is customary to cleanse oneself in a purification fountain called a chōzuya. This act of ritual purification, known as misogi, involves washing one's hands and mouth to purify the body and mind before entering the sacred space.

The spiritual connection to water can also be seen in the tradition of Mizu-iri. Mizu-iri is a ritual in which sacred water drawn from a well, spring, or river is used to infuse objects with spiritual energy. This water is believed to carry the essence of the deity residing in that particular body of water, ensuring the blessings and protection of the spiritual realm. Mizu-iri is often performed during the consecration of new buildings, sacred objects, or during specific events and festivals.

The spiritual landscape of Japan is intricately woven into the fabric of its mythology, connecting humans with the divine through sacred mountains and divine waters. The reverence for these natural elements, and the rituals associated with them, reflect the profound relationship between nature and spirituality in Japanese culture. By exploring these beliefs and traditions, we gain a deeper understanding of the unique spiritual journey that the Japanese people have embarked upon for centuries.

CHAPTER 2: THE PANTHEON OF THE HEAVENS OF JAPANESE MYTHOLOGY

In the vast tapestry of Japanese mythology, the pantheon of heavenly gods holds a significant place. These deities, who reside in the celestial realm, have captivated the hearts and minds of the Japanese people for centuries. Chapter 2 delves into the rich traditions and intricate stories surrounding the heavenly gods of Japanese mythology, offering insight into their origins, roles, and influence on human affairs.

Mythical Origins

Like many ancient mythologies, the roots of Japanese heavenly deities trace back to creation stories. In the beginning, there existed an otherworldly plane known as Takamagahara, the High Plain of Heaven, where the gods resided. This ethereal realm was beyond the reach of mortals and served as the center of cosmic order. Within Takamagahara, the heavenly gods emerged from the primordial forces, Kami, representing the essential life energy of the universe.

Amaterasu, Goddess of the Sun

Among the myriad celestial deities, Amaterasu, the goddess of the sun, stands as one of the most esteemed. Descending from the divine couple Izanagi and Izanami, Amaterasu embodied both light and eternal beauty. She became the ruler of the heavens and bestowed upon the world the gift of light, warmth, and life. The majestic sun goddess held enormous influence over the agricultural cycles, ensuring bountiful harvests and the continued prosperity of the people.

Susano-o, God of Storms and Seas

In stark contrast to the radiant Amaterasu, her brother Susano-o embodied the wild and tempestuous forces of nature. Known as the god of storms and seas, Susano-o brought forth winds, rains, and earthquakes, often triggering chaos and destruction. Despite his turbulent nature, Susano-o played an essential role in Japanese mythology. His adventures and misadventures, such as slaying the serpent Yamata-no-Orochi, were pivotal in shaping the world and the lives of mortals.

A Celestial Compromise

The relationship between Amaterasu and Susano-o epitomizes the delicate balance between order and chaos, light and darkness, in Japanese mythology. One notable tale tells of Susano-o's banishment from Takamagahara after his disruptive behavior, leading him to descend to the mortal realm, known as Ashihara-no-Naka, or the Central Land of Reed Plains. This mythic event established a clear distinction between the mortal world and the realm of the heavenly gods. As a result, Amaterasu and Susano-o's encounters with mortals became pivotal in shaping the course of human history.

The Heavenly Council

Beyond Amaterasu and Susano-o, the heavenly pantheon included a multitude of gods and goddesses, each possessing unique powers and domains. One of the most revered deities within the celestial council was Tsukuyomi, the moon god. Tsukuyomi governed the moon, its phases, and the tides. Legend has it that Tsukuyomi's descent to Earth, an event known as the Tsukinami, led to profound change, including the establishment of the lunar calendar and a deeper understanding of time.

Another influential celestial deity was Susanoo's wife, the goddess Kushinadahime, the epitome of beauty and fertility. She played a crucial role in balancing Susano-o's erratic nature, calming his storms and nurturing the earth. Kushinadahime symbolizes the harmonious connection between the heavens and the terrestrial realm, embodying the reciprocal relationship between the celestial and earthly spheres.

Divine Interactions with Humans

While dwelling in Takamagahara, the heavenly gods frequently interacted with mortals, wielding their powers to shape and influence humankind's destiny. Numerous stories highlight these interactions, underscoring the godly intervention in human affairs. One particularly noteworthy myth is the tale of Ninigi-no-Mikoto, the grandson of Amaterasu. Sent down to Earth with divine treasures, Ninigi became the progenitor of the Japanese imperial line. This connection between the celestial pantheon and the mortal realm solidified the divine origins of the Japanese royal family, lending both prestige and authority.

Chapter 2 has explored the enchanting realm of celestial deities in Japanese mythology. From Amaterasu, the radiant goddess of the sun, to Susano-o, the tempestuous god of storms, these heavenly beings have wielded immeasurable influence on both the celestial and earthly planes. Their interactions with mortals, the delicate balance they maintain, and the stories woven around their lives have shaped the cultural fabric of Japan. In the subsequent chapters, we will continue to unravel the captivating tapestry of mythical beings that grace the annals of Japanese folklore.

Amaterasu: The Sun Goddess and Her Eternal Shine

From the dawn of time, the sun has captivated humanity with its radiant presence, casting its warm light upon the world. Across cultures and civilizations, the sun holds a central place in mythology and folklore, embodying powerful deities that shape the celestial realm. Among these divine figures, none holds a more prominent position and enduring legacy than Amaterasu, the Sun Goddess of Japanese mythology. In this chapter, we delve into the captivating tale of Amaterasu, her eternal shine, and the profound impact she has had on Japanese culture.

In the vast tapestry of Japanese mythology, Amaterasu is considered one of the most essential and revered deities. She is a central figure within the Shinto religion, which holds that the sun is the source of all life. As the ruler of the celestial realm and the heavens, Amaterasu shines her light upon the world, nurturing and sustaining creation.

According to ancient myths, Amaterasu was born from the left eye of her father, Izanagi, as he purified himself after journeying through the underworld. From the moment of her birth, Amaterasu radiated an otherworldly light that illuminated the cosmos. With her pure and gentle energy, she became the embodiment of beauty, goodness, and life itself.

As the myths go, Amaterasu's life took a dramatic turn when her rebellious brother, Susanoo, unleashed chaos and destruction upon the earthly realm. Fearing for her safety and incensed by her brother's actions, Amaterasu retreated into the heavenly sanctuary known as the Ama-no-Iwato. By doing so, she plunged the world into eternal darkness.

Desperate to bring his sister back and restore light to the world, the gods devised a clever plan. They organized a triumphant feast outside the celestial cave, complete with music, dance, and laughter. Curiosity eventually overshadowed Amaterasu's seclusion, and, enticed by the sounds of merry-making, she slowly opened the door to her sanctuary.

As the door crept open, the gods seized the opportunity and quickly placed an enchanted mirror in front of the entrance. As Amaterasu peered out, her own radiant reflection caught her eyes. Mesmerized by her own beauty, she stepped out of the cave, and at that very moment, the gods sealed the entrance behind her.

With her emergence, sunlight once again flooded the world, eradicating the darkness that had lingered for far too long. Thus, Amaterasu's eternal shine was restored, marking her rebirth as the benevolent Sun Goddess.

Amaterasu's radiance extended far beyond the celestial spheres. In ancient Japan, her powerful influence extended over various aspects of life, including agriculture, nurturing growth, and fostering fertility. The belief in Amaterasu's benevolence led to the establishment of Shinto rituals and ceremonies, often centered around the worship of the sun and the gratitude for her divine blessings.

One such notable ceremony is the Jinji Shiki, also known as the Shikinen Sengu, a sacred ritual held every twenty years at the Grand Shrine of Ise. During this ceremony, the shrine and its buildings are rebuilt using traditional techniques and materials, signifying the continuous cycle of life, death, and rebirth. Through these rites and prayers, the people of Japan seek the protection and blessings of Amaterasu, ensuring harmony with nature and divine light in their lives.

Amaterasu's influence can also be seen in the art and literature of Japan. Countless poems, stories, and paintings have been inspired by her ethereal radiance and divine presence. Artists throughout history have captured her beauty in delicate brushstrokes and immortalized her in woodblock prints, evoking a sense of awe and reverence among those who gaze upon her celestial visage.

In addition to her religious and artistic significance, Amaterasu's legends have also shaped the political landscape of Japan. It is said that the imperial lineage of Japan can trace its ancestry back to none other than Amaterasu herself. This belief in a divine connection between the Sun Goddess and the imperial family has permeated Japanese society, cementing the emperor's status as the symbolic descendant of the gods.

Amaterasu's enduring legacy continues to shine brightly in modern-day Japan. From the iconic Japanese flag, featuring a red circle representing the sun, to the country's nickname, "Land of the Rising Sun," the influence of Amaterasu's eternal shine can be felt in every corner of the nation. Her presence reminds the Japanese people of their deep-rooted spirituality, connection to nature, and the eternal cycle of life.

In conclusion, Amaterasu, the Sun Goddess of Japanese mythology, holds an unparalleled place in the hearts and minds of the Japanese people. With her eternal shine, she brings light, life, and beauty to the world. Through her myths, rituals, and artistic representations, Amaterasu's influence reaches far beyond the celestial realm, shaping the culture, spirituality, and identity of Japan. Her story stands as a testament to the enduring power of the sun and our eternal fascination with the divine light that illuminates our lives.

Susanoo: The Tempestuous Storm God

In the pantheon of ancient Japanese mythology, there exists a powerful and enigmatic deity known as Susanoo, the tempestuous storm god. As a prominent figure in the Shinto religion, he represents the untamed forces of nature, simultaneously feared and revered by mortals and fellow gods alike. This chapter delves into the depths of Susanoo's origin, his complex character, and the mythological stories that showcase his tumultuous nature.

Part I: The Birth of Susanoo

According to ancient legends, Susanoo was born from Izanagi, the creator deity, and Izanami, the goddess of creation and death. He emerged from Izanagi's left eye during a purification ritual after his descent into Yomi, the underworld. As a divine being, Susanoo possessed immense power and a tempestuous spirit from the moment of his birth.

Part II: The Tumultuous Nature of Susanoo

From an early age, Susanoo's unpredictable nature was evident. His fiery disposition often led him to be associated with violent storms, typhoons, and other forms of chaotic weather. The myths surrounding Susanoo's interactions with his siblings, Amaterasu, the sun goddess, and Tsukuyomi, the moon god, further illustrate his volatile character.

One fateful encounter tells the tale of Susanoo's clash with his sister Amaterasu. Driven by jealousy, he wreaked havoc and destruction in the celestial realm, compelling Amaterasu to retreat to a cave, casting the world into darkness. It took the efforts of other gods and elaborate antics to coax Amaterasu out of seclusion and restore light to the world. This tale symbolizes the eternal cycle of light and darkness, and the delicate balance between chaos and harmony that Susanoo represents.

Part III: Susanoo's Quest for Transformation

Despite his impulsive and erratic nature, Susanoo possessed a desire for self-improvement, seeking to overcome his flaws and forge a new path. One of the most famous mythological episodes involving Susanoo describes his encounter with a monstrous eight-headed serpent named Yamata no Orochi.

In this tale, Susanoo met an elderly couple grieving their impending sacrifice to the fearsome Orochi. Recognizing a chance to prove himself and rid the land of the terror, Susanoo offered his assistance. He devised a cunning plan, setting eight massive sake barrels as bait, each filled with the potent alcoholic beverage. Orochi, enticed by the intoxicating aroma, consumed the barrels, becoming inebriated and vulnerable. Taking advantage of the serpent's stupor, Susanoo slew

Orochi, rescuing the couple and freeing the land from its threat.

Part IV: Susanoo's Exile

Despite his heroic triumph against Orochi, Susanoo's uncontrollable acts of destruction continued, prompting the other gods to question his place among them. In one particularly calamitous incident, Susanoo desecrated a paddy field that belonged to Amaterasu, ruining the crops that sustained the people. Enraged, Amaterasu declared Susanoo an outcast and forever banished him from the celestial realm.

With his banishment in effect, Susanoo descended to the mortal realm and wandered aimlessly, lost in his own remorse. This period of exile further reflects the growth and introspection that Susanoo undergoes during his journey, allowing him to develop a newfound understanding of his own strength, weaknesses, and the consequences of his actions.

Part V: Susanoo's Redemption and Legacy

During his exile, Susanoo encountered an elderly couple weaving cloth beneath a mulberry tree. Mired in poverty and despair, they explained that they had fallen on hard times due to a lack of children. Touched by their plight, Susanoo offered assistance, providing them with instructions on weaving patterns and praying to the gods for guidance. Soon after, the couple discovered a gift left by the gods, a bundle of cloth. Unraveling it, they found treasures within, elevating their lives from destitution to prosperity.

Impressed by Susanoo's compassion and newfound wisdom, the gods ultimately forgave him and reinstated him as a deity. Susanoo's redemption marked a significant turning point in his story, emphasizing the potential for growth and transformation, even for seemingly unredeemable characters.

As time went on, tales of Susanoo's exploits spread throughout ancient Japan, cementing his place as a complex and influential deity. The stories surrounding Susanoo not only entertained and captivated listeners but also served as cautionary tales, reminding mortals of the perils of uncontrolled emotions and the importance of seeking growth and self-betterment.

And so, Susanoo the tempestuous storm god, with his fiery temper, volatile nature, and ultimate redemption, remains one of the most fascinating figures in ancient Japanese mythology. As we explore the pantheon of deities and their intricate stories, we find a reflection of the human experience – our struggles, desires, and potential for growth. Susanoo's tale is a reminder that even in the most tempestuous storms, there lies an opportunity for transformation and eventual redemption.

Tsukuyomi: The Moon God's Silent Gaze

The ethereal glow of the full moon bathed the land as a celestial presence loomed above. It was Tsukuyomi, the majestic moon god, casting his silent gaze upon the world below. The people held their breath in anticipation, for this was a rare occurrence—a moment when the heavens revealed their secrets, an opportunity to peer into the divine.

Tsukuyomi was a figure shrouded in mystique, known for his serenity and enigmatic persona. Legend had it that he emerged from the body of Izanagi, the creator god, when he washed his face after returning from the underworld. Each night, Tsukuyomi ascended to the skies, traversing the celestial realm with grace and purpose.

As the embodiment of the moon, Tsukuyomi possessed an otherworldly beauty. His silver hair cascaded down his back like a flowing river, blending seamlessly with the night sky. His piercing azure eyes mirrored the secrets of the cosmos, a reflection of the heavens themselves. The god's luminous visage seemed to glow softly, illuminating the darkest corners of the world below.

The moon's benevolent light spread across the land, casting long, eerie shadows and revealing hidden wonders. In the dead of night, creatures seldom seen emerged from their hidden abodes.

Tsukuyomi observed with a detached fascination as the nocturnal animals stirred, awed by their uncanny ability to navigate the darkness.

But it was not only creatures of the night that felt the divine presence of Tsukuyomi. Humans, too, believed in his power and significance. They whispered tales of divine intervention and forged an unbreakable bond with the moon god. In their eyes, Tsukuyomi represented a guiding light, a beacon of hope amidst the chaos of existence.

Stories about Tsukuyomi's ability to heal the wounded and cure ailments had been passed down through generations. It was believed that anyone blessed by his touch would be granted instant relief from pain and suffering. People shared tales of miraculous healings, sparking a desperate longing in those afflicted by illness or injury. They yearned for a chance to stand beneath the moonlight, craving the touch of divine solace.

The moon god's influence transcended the physical realm. His gaze, silent and distant, bestowed wisdom upon those who humbly sought it. Many claimed to have received visions, heard whispered guidance in their dreams, or stumbled upon life-altering revelations whenever Tsukuyomi's gaze fell upon them. These incidents birthed the belief that the moon god had the power to bestow enlightenment upon mortals, offering a glimpse into the celestial tapestry of existence.

Yet, with all his mythical elegance, Tsukuyomi remained a solitary figure. His ethereal countenance, though captivating, seemed at times detached from humanity. The people marveled at his beauty but couldn't help but wonder if the god even noticed their existence. His silent gaze, while awe-inspiring, often left them longing for more profound connections with the divine.

Tsukuyomi was far from oblivious to the desires of mortals; he understood their yearning for a tangible connection. However, he was aware of the delicate balance that needed to be upheld. Too much interference, and the cycle of life and death would falter, leading to chaos and disharmony. He chose to watch the world from afar, ensuring that his presence remained a catalyst for growth and introspection.

It was beneath the moonlight that Tsukuyomi's presence felt most palpable. The serene brilliance of the full moon stirred emotions and deep contemplation within those who dared to gaze into its cytoplasmic reflection. Lovers found solace in its glow, embracing beneath its luminescence, professing heartfelt declarations and sealing promises with a kiss, forever etched into the ethereal realm.

Artists sought inspiration, captivated by the moon god's enchanting allure. They defied the boundaries of human creativity, capturing the essence of Tsukuyomi's divine radiance on canvas or in lyrical compositions. Through their craft, they sought to immortalize his silent gaze, bridging the gap between mortal and divine, and leaving behind a legacy that would transcend time.

Though Tsukuyomi's influence had endured for countless millennia, the moon god remained a mysterious enigma. His silent gaze continued to captivate the hearts and minds of those fortunate enough to witness its majesty. People yearned for the secrets that lay hidden within his depths, for they believed that understanding Tsukuyomi's essence would bring them closer to comprehending the intricate nature of their own existence.

As the night wore on, the moon began its gradual descent, fading gracefully into the horizon. Tsukuyomi's presence became less tangible, his connection to the mortal realm slipping away until only a wistful memory remained. But the impact he left on the world was immeasurable, woven into the fabric of human consciousness, forever immortalized in tales and legends.

And so, as the moon waned, the people bid farewell, their hearts filled with gratitude and reverence for Tsukuyomi, the moon god's silent gaze. They found solace in knowing that, although his presence was fleeting, the moon, with all its serene beauty, would continue to shine upon them, illuminating their paths until the end of days.

Izanami and Izanagi: The Celestial Duo of Creation

In the vast expanse of the celestial realm, there resides a sacred duo whose union brought about the very existence of our mortal world. Izanami and Izanagi, the celestial duo of creation, stand at the heart of Japanese mythology, weaving a tapestry of divine power and cosmic harmony. Through their harmonious union, the heavens were separated from the earth, giving birth to countless deities and shaping the destiny of humanity.

Legend has it that before the existence of the physical world, there was only a shapeless and chaotic mass. Within this formless void, Izanami and Izanagi emerged, their ethereal presence radiating with the promise of creation. Floating above the tumultuous abyss, they beheld one another and from that intimate meeting, the universe began to take form.

Izanami, the goddess of creation and death, was a radiant and enigmatic figure. Her delicate beauty was matched only by her immense power, for she held dominion over all aspects of creation, from the majestic mountains to the smallest blade of grass. Her noble and dignified demeanor inspired awe in all who beheld her, as she commanded reverence and respect from both mortals and gods alike. With a graceful wave of her hand, she brought forth the gentle rains and the bountiful harvests, nurturing the earth with her limitless generosity.

On the other hand, Izanagi embodied the essence of the divine masculine. Possessing an aura of strength and wisdom, he was the ever-watchful guardian of creation. His form was resplendent, his countenance bearing witness to the immense power he commanded. With his shimmering sword in hand, he served as a faithful companion to Izanami, his actions guided by an unwavering sense of duty and honor. It was through his efforts that order was brought forth amid the chaos, allowing the celestial duo to shape the destinies of both gods and humans.

But it was their union that truly defined their divine purpose, for it was in their sacred embrace that the world came into being. As they circled around a celestial pillar, swirling vortexes of energy erupted, tearing apart the formless void. From the separation of heaven and earth, the island of Japan was born, its rugged landscapes and serene beauty serving as a testament to their divine creativity. Mountains pierced through the heavens, rivers flowed with laughter, and the gentle rustling of leaves whispered tales of their celestial union.

Fueled by an insatiable desire to create life, Izanami and Izanagi descended from the heavens to the newly formed earth. As their ethereal feet touched the fertile soil, they found themselves immersed in a world teeming with untapped potential. Fired with the energy borne of their love, they embarked on a mission to bring life and order to this nascent realm.

With a divine spear, Izanagi pierced the earth, and from the gushing depths emerged the crystalline waters of the sea. As the sacred waters caressed the land, they gave birth to grand oceans, teeming with life and mysteries yet to be discovered. Breathing life into the inert earth, Izanami scattered seeds across the fertile plains, from which sprouted a tapestry of colors and fragrances. The celestial duo reveled in their creation, each act of divine intervention revealing new wonders to be cherished.

Yet, their celestial harmony was disrupted when tragedy befell Izanami. As the goddess of death, she bore within her the ultimate symbol of life's fragility. During the birth of their child, she suffered a grievous wound, pushing her towards the precipice of the underworld. Overwhelmed by grief, Izanagi embarked on a desperate journey to reunite with his beloved, determined to rescue her from the realm of death.

But the underworld beckoned with treacherous allure, the infinite darkness consuming all who dared to traverse its depths. As Izanagi ventured further, he encountered the grisly forms of the dead, their tormented souls haunting the desolate realm. Eventually, he discovered Izanami, but the reunion was far from joyous. The once vibrant goddess had been reduced to a spectral entity, her beauty marred by the ashen pallor of death. In her despair, she requested that Izanagi not gaze upon her decaying visage, a command he reluctantly obeyed.

As Izanagi sought to escape from the underworld, Izanami's anguish transformed into rage. She vowed to take a thousand lives every day, cursing the living with the pain and agony she experienced. Fleeing in terror, Izanagi barely managed to escape by sealing the entrance to the underworld with a massive boulder. Collapsing at its base, he emerged into the world of the living, a solemn reminder of the price one pays for defying the natural order.

This tragic tale of love, loss, and sacrifice serves as a reminder of the delicate balance between creation and death. Izanami and Izanagi, the celestial duo of creation, bestowed upon the world its greatest gift - the cycles of birth and rebirth. Through their divine love, they offered humanity a chance to flourish and evolve, their creative energy continuing to shape the world long after their presence ceased to be.

Thus, their story reverberates through the annals of time, a testament to the eternal nature of creation and the profound impact celestial beings have upon the human experience. Whether we look to the heavens to seek guidance or find solace in the wonders of nature, the influence of Izanami and Izanagi continues to resonate within our collective consciousness, reminding us of the enduring power of creation and the bonds that unite us all.

CHAPTER 3: SPIRITS AND SUPERNATURAL BEINGS

Japanese mythology is an intricate web of stories, rituals, and beliefs that paint a vivid picture of the spirit world. Central to this cosmos are a variety of supernatural beings, ranging from revered deities to enigmatic creatures, that have shaped the nation's cultural, spiritual, and everyday life for millennia.

Kami: The term "kami" often gets translated as "god," but this doesn't fully encompass its essence. Kami can be deities, but they can also be spirits of nature—trees, rivers, mountains—and even departed ancestors. They're intrinsic to Shinto, Japan's indigenous religion, emphasizing the divine in nature and the harmonious relationship between the spiritual and physical realms. Worshiping kami often involves rituals at shrines and offerings to show respect and seek blessings.

Yokai: The realm of yokai is vast and varied. These creatures and spirits can be malevolent, benevolent, or neutral. Some, like the playful tanuki with its shape-shifting abilities or the mischievous kappa dwelling in rivers, have become popular characters in folklore and modern media. Others, like the umbrella-turned-monster "kasaobake", serve as reminders of the mystery and wonder in everyday objects.

Oni: Often depicted as horned demons wielding clubs, oni are fearsome creatures prominent in Japanese folklore. While they're typically seen as malevolent, some tales depict them in a more sympathetic or even protective light.

Onryo: These are vengeful spirits, usually of those who experienced deep jealousy or were wronged in life. Their anger carries into the afterlife, and they're believed to cause harm in the world of the living. The story of Oiwa, a woman betrayed and disfigured by her husband, is a classic tale of an onryo.

Tengu: Bird-like creatures dwelling in mountains, tengu are considered both protectors and punishers. They're associated with the Shugendo tradition of mountain asceticism and are often seen as both harbingers of war and protectors of forests and Buddhist teachings.

Dragons and Serpents: Unlike their Western counterparts, Japanese dragons are primarily water deities, often benevolent and associated with rainfall and bodies of water. The tale of the white serpent in Lake Biwa is a love story between a man and a serpent-turned-woman, highlighting the theme of transformation common in many of these myths.

Kodama: These are tree spirits, emphasizing the sacredness of trees in Shinto belief. Cutting down a tree housing a kodama can bring misfortune, further emphasizing the balance between human needs and respect for nature.

In essence, spirits and supernatural beings in Japanese mythology are not just characters in old tales but reflections of the nation's values, fears, hopes, and understanding of the universe.

They bridge the tangible and intangible, reminding us of the delicate balance between humans and the world around us.

Whether feared or revered, these entities continue to be significant in Japanese culture, influencing art, literature, and daily practices.

Kitsune: The Cunning Foxes of Mythical Japan

In the realm of Japanese folklore, amidst the tapestry of fantastical creatures and mythical beings, one creature stands out for its cunning and mesmerizing allure - the Kitsune. Translated as "fox" in Japanese, the Kitsune holds a significant place in the country's cultural heritage, appearing in various forms across literature, art, and religious beliefs. These foxes, believed to possess magical powers and shape-shifting abilities, continue to captivate our imagination with their complex nature and multifaceted character.

Origins and Early References

The origins of the Kitsune can be traced back to ancient Japan, where foxes were considered animals of mystery and supernatural power. Although the exact time of their origin is shrouded in the mists of time, the earliest references to the Kitsune can be found in the Nihon Shoki (The Chronicles of Japan), written in the 8th century. It is here that the Kitsune appears for the first time as shape-shifters, often assuming the form of beautiful women to deceive humans.

Through the Ages: The Many Faces of Kitsune

Throughout the centuries, the Kitsune took on various roles and personas, becoming an integral part of Japanese folklore. They are known to possess incredible knowledge, magical abilities, and an inherent wisdom that both fascinates and frightens humans. Kitsune can change their appearance at will, shifting from a small fox to a seductive woman or even a mighty tree. This shapeshifting has been depicted in countless tales, where the Kitsune assumes different forms to interact with humans, often testing their morality and cunning.

One of the many forms a Kitsune can take on is that of a yōkai, a supernatural creature driven to interact and sometimes haunt humans. These yōkai Kitsune are often described as mischievous, playing pranks on unsuspecting villagers or causing havoc in the form of fire or illusions. While some Kitsune are playful and trickster-like, others have more sinister intentions, feeding off human emotions such as jealousy, anger, or desire. These malevolent foxes, known as the nogitsune, are regarded with caution and fear.

However, not all Kitsune are mischievous or malevolent. Some are benevolent and play a guardian role in the lives of humans. In such cases, they are often associated with Inari, the Shinto kami (deity) of rice, fertility, and agriculture. It is believed that these benevolent Kitsune serve as messengers of Inari, showering blessings upon the faithful.

Cultural Significance and Symbolism

The Kitsune's multifaceted nature and distinctive characteristics have led to its deep-rooted presence in Japanese culture. From literature to art and even modern-day anime, the Kitsune has cemented its position as an iconic symbol of Japan.

In Japanese literature, the Kitsune plays a prominent role. The medieval collection of stories called the Konjaku Monogatari features many tales centered around these enchanting foxes. One famous story tells of a nobleman who falls in love with a beautiful woman, only to discover later that she was a Kitsune in disguise. This narrative highlights the Kitsune's seductive power and the importance of discernment and trust in human relationships.

Artists throughout history have also been captivated by the intricate beauty of the Kitsune, portraying them in paintings, woodblock prints, and sculptures. These depictions often emphasize both the Kitsune's fox-like qualities and their human-like expressions, blurring the boundary between the supernatural and the mortal world.

Beyond art and literature, the Kitsune has also found its way into modern pop culture, sparking the imagination of countless creators worldwide. In manga and anime, Kitsune characters frequently appear, reflecting their cunning and captivating personas. Their allure continues to inspire and fascinate a global audience, transcending cultural boundaries through their representation in popular media.

The Kitsune's Influence on Spirituality

The Kitsune's influence extends beyond folklore and cultural symbolism and intersects with spiritual beliefs. In Shintoism, the indigenous religion of Japan, the Kitsune is closely associated with Inari, one of the most widely worshiped kami. Temples dedicated to Inari often feature stone fox statues guarding the entrance, representing the Kitsune as the deity's messengers and protectors. The Kitsune's connection to Inari is believed to grant them powers of fertility, prosperity, and protection from agricultural disasters. People often leave offerings of food, particularly fried tofu, to honor the Kitsune as they believe it is their favorite food. Moreover, fox possession, a state in which humans are believed to be taken over by the spirit of a Kitsune, is considered a form of divine possession by some followers of Shintoism.

As the realm of Japanese folklore reveals its enchanting spectacles, the cunning and elusive Kitsune undoubtedly stand out amongst the mystical creatures. Their shape-shifting abilities, mischievous pranks, and beguiling allure have infused Japanese culture for centuries, leaving an indelible mark on literature, art, and religious beliefs.

The Kitsune's ability to straddle the line between human and supernatural, mischief and protection, good and evil, makes them a captivating subject worthy of exploration. Their stories and symbolism continue to be retold, ensuring that the legacy of the Kitsune endures, captivating the hearts and imagination of generations to come. So, let us delve into the enigmatic realm of the Kitsune, where fox and fantasy seamlessly intertwine.

Tengu: The Mystical Bird-like Protectors

Throughout the rich tapestry of Japanese folklore and mythology, there exist a multitude of fascinating creatures and entities, each possessing their own unique powers, abilities, and purpose. One among these remarkable beings is the enigmatic and beguiling Tengu. With their bird-like features and extraordinary abilities, Tengu have captured the imaginations of people for centuries, embodying both awe and fear. In this chapter, we shall embark on a journey to explore the realm of Tengu, diving into their origins, characteristics, and role as mystical protectors.

1. Origins and Legends of Tengu:

To understand the essence of Tengu, we must delve into their mythological roots and uncover the legends that surround their creation. In Japanese folklore, Tengu are often depicted as beings born from the merger of human and bird, taking on avian characteristics whilst retaining human-like forms. They are believed to dwell deep in the mountains, secluded from the hustle and bustle of human civilization.

The origins of Tengu can be traced back to the 9th century, during the Heian period, where they first emerged in Buddhist and Shinto traditions. They were initially regarded as disruptive and malevolent spirits, haunting mountain monasteries and tormenting unsuspecting monks. However, over time, the perception of Tengu evolved, and they began to be seen as protectors of the Dharma, the teachings of Buddhism.

2. The Physical Form of Tengu:

Tengu are often depicted in visual arts and literature as having a distinct appearance that sets them apart from other mythological creatures. They possess a humanoid body with bird-like attributes, most commonly displayed through their wings and beaked face. Tengu are primarily associated with long-nosed masks, which have become synonymous with their existence. These masks, known as "tengu-men," not only serve as a visual representation but are believed to carry mystical powers, symbolizing omnipresence and wisdom.

Tengu are also renowned for their ability to change their physical shape at will. One particular form they can assume is that of a large bird, resembling a crow or a hawk. This form grants them the powers of flight and swift movement, allowing them to traverse great distances in the blink of an eye.

3. The Powers and Abilities of Tengu:

Beyond their distinctive appearance, Tengu possess a wide range of extraordinary powers and abilities that further add to their mystique. These powers often vary depending on the region and specific legends associated with each Tengu clan. However, some common abilities attributed to Tengu include:

- Astounding Martial Prowess: Tengu are renowned for their prowess in various forms of combat, excelling in swordsmanship and archery. Their skill with the sword is often said to be unrivaled, and their arrows seldom miss their targets.

- Shape-Shifting: As mentioned earlier, Tengu have the power to transform their physical form, allowing them to appear either as humans, birds, or a combination of both. This ability grants them unmatched versatility and an advantage in certain situations.

- Control over Natural Elements: Tengu are believed to have dominion over wind and the natural forces, enabling them to conjure powerful gusts, create storms, or whisk themselves away in a whirlwind.

- Telepathy and Mind Control: Tengu possess the ability to communicate telepathically with humans and sway the minds of others to fulfill their objectives. This skill can be used for both positive and negative purposes, depending on the intentions of the Tengu in question.

These exceptional abilities lend Tengu an air of invincibility and inspire awe and reverence among those who encounter them.

4. The Role of Tengu as Protectors:

While Tengu were initially depicted as malevolent spirits, their role gradually shifted to that of protectors and defenders. Japanese folklore often recounts tales of Tengu intervening in human affairs, aiding individuals who walk the path of righteousness and thwarting those who seek to do harm. They are believed to possess an innate sense of justice, bringing balance to the world and safeguarding the moral order.

One notable tale tells of the Tengu warrior Sōjōbō, leader of the Tengu on Mount Kurama. Sōjōbō took young warriors under his wing, instructing them in the ways of combat and nurturing their spiritual and physical prowess. These students, known as the Tengu's pupils, became formidable warriors and defenders of justice in their own right, continuing the legacy of their avian mentors.

The idea of Tengu as protectors goes beyond individual interactions. In Japanese spiritual beliefs, Tengu are seen as guardians of the deep mountains and sacred forests, ensuring harmony and protecting the natural world from harm. They are considered allies of the gods, acting as sentinels of the heavens and maintaining a spiritual balance between the earthly realm and the divine.

5. The Encounter with Tengu:

Though rare, encounters with Tengu have been reported throughout history, often leaving those who witness them in awe and disbelief. The legends and tales surrounding these mystical beings serve as inspiration for those who seek enlightenment and guidance on their own spiritual journey.

Most encounters with Tengu occur in sacred and secluded places, such as deep mountain valleys or hidden shrines. There, seekers of spiritual wisdom may find themselves face to face with Tengu, who will impart ancient teachings, profound insights, or issue trials to test the resilience and dedication of those who seek their counsel. These interactions can be life-changing, bestowing individuals with great wisdom and fortitude for their future endeavors.

As we conclude this chapter on Tengu - the mystical bird-like protectors, we have merely scratched the surface of their vast lore and intriguing nature. These enigmatic beings, born from the union of human and bird, embody an aura of mystery, wisdom, and power. From their evolving role in Japanese folklore to their awe-inspiring abilities as protectors and guardians, Tengu continue to captivate the human imagination. As we venture further into the realm of Japanese mythology, we shall uncover more intriguing secrets, discovering the interconnectedness of these beings and the profound impact they have had on culture and society.

Kappa: Mischievous Water Spirits and Their Legends

In the vast realm of folklore and mythology, one encounters a diverse array of mysterious and captivating creatures. Among the most intriguing are the Kappa, legendary water spirits found in Japanese folklore. These enigmatic beings have been a subject of fascination and awe for centuries. Known for their mischievous nature and powerful presence, Kappa have captivated the imaginations of countless generations with their unique characteristics and legends.

Origins and Legends

The origins of the Kappa can be traced back to ancient Japan, where they were believed to inhabit rivers, lakes, and other bodies of water. These mythical creatures were often described as humanoid in appearance, possessing webbed hands and feet, scaly skin, and a curious dome-shaped head filled with water. This water-filled cavity was said to be the source of their power and vitality. Kappa legends were interwoven into the rich tapestry of Japanese folklore and have been passed down through generations.

One of the most widely known legends involving Kappa takes place in a small village nestled amidst serene rice paddies. It is said that during a hot summer, Hiroshi, a skilled archer, ventured to the local pond seeking relief from the scorching sun. Unbeknownst to Hiroshi, the pond was the dwelling place of a mischievous Kappa named Kaito.

As Hiroshi dove into the cool waters, he inadvertently disturbed the slumber of the Kappa. Outraged by this intrusion, Kaito surfaced from the depths to confront Hiroshi. The Kappa, renowned for their martial arts prowess, challenged the archer to a duel, seeking to overpower the insolent human.

However, Hiroshi, skilled in archery and combat, proved to be an equally formidable opponent. The battle between them raged on, reaching a climax as Kaito attempted to drag Hiroshi into the water. Yet, utilizing his wit and strength, Hiroshi managed to outsmart the Kappa by bowing deeply, causing his opponent to involuntarily return the gesture. This caused Kaito's vital water to leak from his head, rendering him weak and vulnerable.

Realizing the Kappa's weakened state, Hiroshi quickly grabbed a nearby bamboo container and filled it with pond water, offering it to the Kappa in a gesture of goodwill. Touched by Hiroshi's compassion, Kaito regained his strength and pledged to protect the village from any harm. From that day forward, the waters of the pond were regarded as sacred, with Hiroshi and Kaito's tale becoming a cherished local legend.

Characteristics and Traits

Kappa are renowned for their unique physical and behavioral traits. Other than their distinctive physical appearance, including their webbed extremities and water-filled head cavity, Kappa are known for their mischievous nature and trickster tendencies. Most often, they are portrayed as child-sized beings with a variety of supernatural abilities.

One remarkable ability possessed by Kappa is their knack for mastering various martial arts. Known to rival even the most skilled human combatants, Kappa employ techniques that combine agility, strength, and cunning. Their skill allows them to outmaneuver their opponents and manipulate water to their advantage.

Another prominent characteristic of Kappa is their obsession with politeness and respect in Japanese society. It is believed that if one bows deeply to a Kappa, the water within their head cavity will spill out, causing the Kappa to lose its energy and strength. This reverence for social etiquette often plays a crucial role in legends and encounters with Kappa, as demonstrated in Hiroshi and Kaito's tale.

Mischievous and Prankster Nature

While Kappa are not inherently malevolent beings, their mischievous nature often leads them to wreak havoc on humanity. These water spirits possess an insatiable desire to play pranks and engage in various antics, both harmless and occasionally harmful. From unsettling fishermen's boats to creating alliances with monkeys to deceive unsuspecting travelers, Kappa have gained a reputation for their tricks.

A common prank attributed to Kappa involves engaging in sumo wrestling matches with unsuspecting victims. These challenges typically occur near bodies of water, where the Kappa's aquatic advantages come into play. They entice their opponent into grappling with them, utilizing their superior strength and skills to overpower them. However, by displaying humility and respect through a deep bow, one can defeat a Kappa in combat, as Hiroshi did with Kaito.

Modern Cultural Influence

The legends surrounding Kappa continue to captivate the Japanese imagination and have permeated various aspects of modern-day culture. Their influence can be seen in numerous forms of media, such as literature, films, and even video games. Often depicted as both fearsome adversaries and comical characters, the Kappa's legacy has proven enduring and ingrained within Japanese society.

In popular culture, Kappa have appeared in films such as "The Great Yokai War" and "Tam Warner Kappa World." These movies showcase the variety of personalities and roles that Kappa characters can assume, from allies aiding the protagonists to cunning antagonists plotting schemes.

Moreover, the video game industry has embraced the allure of Kappa, gracing numerous gaming titles with their presence. A prominent example is the iconic Nintendo franchise, Super Mario, where Kappa make appearances as both boss battles and helpful allies. This further emphasizes the continuing popularity of Kappa legends and their integration into modern entertainment.

The enduring legends of Kappa, mischievous water spirits, have fascinated and captivated generations of Japanese people. With their distinctive physical appearance, iconic traits, and mischievous tendencies, Kappa have become an integral part of Japanese folklore and culture. Their mythical tales continue to inspire awe and wonder, from their martial arts prowess to their relationship with humans based on respect and etiquette. As these legends live on through various forms of media, the enigmatic allure of Kappa ensures their place in the rich tapestry of Japanese mythology.

Oni: The Fearsome Demons of Japanese Folklore

In the vast tapestry of Japanese folklore, there exists a group of mythical creatures that strike fear into the hearts of many - the Oni. These fearsome demons have long captured the imagination of the Japanese people, embodying both terror and fascination. From their gruesome appearances to their legendary strength, Oni have become an integral part of Japan's rich cultural heritage. In this chapter, we delve into the captivating world of Oni, exploring their origins, characteristic features, and their role in Japanese folklore.

1. Legends and Origins

To understand the true nature of the Oni, we must first explore their origins. As with many mythical creatures, Oni's origins lie in ancient folklore and legends passed down through generations. According to Japanese tradition, Oni are said to be the embodiment of evil spirits or Yokai, emerging from the underworld to wreak havoc on the surface world.

The earliest mentions of Oni can be found in the Kojiki and Nihon Shoki, two ancient chronicles that document Japan's history and mythology. These texts describe Oni as terrifying beings with fearsome appearances, often depicted as large humanoid creatures with devilish traits such as horns, sharp fangs, and wild, unkempt hair. The Oni's skin is often painted in vibrant hues of blue or red, adding to their menacing aura.

2. Features and Characteristics

One cannot discuss Oni without mentioning their distinct features and characteristic traits. Apart from their physical appearance, Oni are known for their formidable strength and heightened abilities. These demons possess superhuman strength, capable of lifting enormous boulders and wreaking havoc with a single swipe of their massive club-like weapons.

Furthermore, Oni are often associated with their immense size. They tower over ordinary humans, standing anywhere between seven to ten feet tall. Their muscular frames and bulging veins only serve to emphasize the terror they inspire. Despite their size, Oni are believed to possess a remarkable speed and agility, making it nearly impossible to outrun these fearsome creatures once they set their sights on their prey.

Another notable feature of Oni is their unruly behavior. They are notorious for their fiery tempers and relentless pursuit of mischief and chaos. It is said that Oni take pleasure in tormenting humans, especially those who have committed wicked deeds. They revel in the suffering of others, often employing their insidious cunning to bring misery upon their victims.

3. Oni in Folklore and Popular Culture

Throughout the centuries, Oni have played a significant role in Japanese folklore, appearing in various tales, plays, and artworks. They are often depicted as malevolent beings lurking in forests, remote mountains, or dark caves. In many folk tales, Oni serve as antagonists, causing mayhem and hardship for the protagonists, who must find ways to outwit or defeat these formidable adversaries.

One popular story featuring Oni is the famous folk tale Momotaro, or "Peach Boy." In this narrative, a boy born from a peach embarks on a journey to defeat a group of marauding Oni terrorizing the local villages. With the help of his animal companions, Momotaro takes on the Oni and emerges victorious, symbolizing the triumph of good over evil.

In addition to their presence in folklore, Oni have made their way into various forms of popular culture. They frequently appear in traditional Japanese theater, such as Noh and Kabuki, where actors don vivid costumes and masks to bring these fearsome demons to life. Oni also play prominent roles in modern manga, anime, and video games, captivating audiences worldwide with their iconic appearances and sinister personas.

4. The Symbolism of Oni

Behind their terrifying exterior, Oni hold a deeper symbolic meaning within Japanese culture. These demons often represent the embodiment of human flaws, desires, and vices. They serve as cautionary figures, warning against the consequences of succumbing to negative emotions and immoral behavior.

In Japanese mythology, Oni are also associated with spiritual and supernatural elements. They are viewed as powerful guardian figures, capable of warding off malicious spirits and protecting sacred places. Shrines and temples are often adorned with statues or paintings of Oni, serving as a visual deterrent against evil forces.

5. Rituals and Festivals

It would be remiss to discuss Oni without mentioning the vibrant festivals and rituals dedicated to these demons. One such festival is Setsubun, which occurs yearly on February 3rd. During this event, people gather to cast out evil spirits and invite good fortune by throwing dried soybeans at someone wearing a devilish Oni mask and shouting, "Oni wa soto, fuku wa uchi!" (Out with the demons, in with good luck!).

Similarly, the Hadaka Matsuri, or Naked Festival, held in various regions across Japan, features participants wearing only loincloths and daubing themselves with mud to resemble Oni. This unique festival celebrates the triumph over evil and encourages participants to cast their fears aside.

6. Legacy and Influence

The legacy of the Oni in Japanese folklore continues to thrive to this day. Their frightening visage and mythological status make them subjects of fascination for both locals and tourists alike. Oni continue to inspire artists, writers, and filmmakers, serving as a wellspring of creativity and imaginative storytelling.

Beyond their artistic influence, Oni's presence extends to contemporary society, where their image is often used to ward off evil spirits. Talismans and charms, adorned with Oni motifs, can be found in homes, vehicles, and businesses, believed to provide protection against malevolent forces.

In conclusion, the Oni demons stand as captivating figures in Japanese folklore, captivating the imaginations of generations. Their monstrous appearances, immense strength, and notorious mischief make them both feared and admired. From their origins in ancient legends to their role in rituals and festivals, the Oni's legacy endures, leaving an indelible mark on Japan's cultural landscape. As we delve into the enchanting world of Japanese folklore, the Oni demons take their rightful place as intriguing characters in this tapestry of mythical beings.

CHAPTER 4: SACRED SITES AND SPIRITUAL JOURNEYS

In the realm of Japanese mythology, sacred sites hold immense importance, serving as the spiritual bridge between mortals and deities. These enchanted places have captivated the hearts and minds of countless generations, becoming the backdrop for awe-inspiring spiritual journeys and captivating tales. In this chapter, we will embark on a mystical exploration of the sacred sites and their profound significance within Japanese mythology. From ancient temples nestled in tranquil valleys to sacred mountains revered as the dwelling places of gods, we will delve into the captivating realm of spiritual pilgrimage.

1. The Enchanted Temple of Ise:

Nestled in the dense forests of Mie Prefecture, the Ise Grand Shrine, or Ise Jingu, stands as a testament to the inherent spirituality of Japanese mythology. This sacred shrine complex comprises two main shrines, the Inner Shrine, or Naiku, and the Outer Shrine, or Geku. Shrouded in an air of mystery and awe, Ise Jingu has remained a pilgrim's destination since time immemorial. Ancient chronicles and legends speak of the shrine's mythical origins, with tales of its establishment by the sun goddess, Amaterasu.

Visiting Ise Jingu is not merely an act of devotion but also an opportunity for spiritual renewal. The journey toward Ise is often considered a pilgrimage of the soul, where one leaves behind worldly concerns to seek solace and enlightenment. As pilgrims approach the main shrines, they encounter long, stone-lined paths flanked by towering ancient trees, evoking a sense of sacredness and reverence. The rituals surrounding the maintenance and rebuilding of Ise Jingu serve as a profound reminder of the cyclical nature of existence and the impermanence of all things.

2. The Sacred Mountain of Mount Fuji:

No exploration of sacred sites in Japanese mythology would be complete without a journey to Mount Fuji, the iconic and sacred mountain that captivates both locals and foreigners alike. Revered as a dwelling place of gods and a path to enlightenment, Mount Fuji holds deep spiritual significance in Shinto and Buddhist traditions. Its majestic presence has inspired artists, poets, and pilgrims for centuries.

Mount Fuji's spiritual allure lies not only in its towering figure but also in the arduous journey undertaken by those who seek its summit. Climbing Mount Fuji is seen as an act of self-discovery and discipline, a physical and spiritual journey to overcome one's limitations and confront the divine. Pilgrims ascend the mountain during the summer months, braving treacherous paths and unpredictable weather conditions, all the while meditating on the impermanence of life and the ephemeral nature of existence.

3. The Mystical Island of Okinoshima:

Tucked away in the Sea of Japan, the island of Okinoshima remains one of Japan's most enigmatic and sacred sites. Designated as a UNESCO World Heritage Site, Okinoshima is known for its pristine beauty and spiritual significance. Access to the island is restricted, and only a select few are granted permission to set foot upon its hallowed grounds.

Okinoshima serves as a focal point for rituals and offerings dedicated to the gods. Legend has it that the island was created as a dwelling place for the gods of the sea. A visit to Okinoshima is not just a pilgrimage; it requires deep respect and reverence for the sacredness of the land. The island's rituals center around the veneration of the goddess of the sea, symbolizing the delicate balance between humans and nature.

4. The Mysterious Power of Kumano:

Located on the Kii Peninsula, Kumano has been regarded as a sacred site since ancient times. The Kumano Sanzan, a group of three grand shrines—Kumano Hongu Taisha, Kumano Nachi Taisha, and Kumano Hayatama Taisha—form the core of the Kumano pilgrimage route.

This spiritual journey, known as the Kumano Kodo, takes pilgrims through dense forests, picturesque mountains, and serene rivers.

The Kumano pilgrimage is not merely a physical endeavor but a transformative experience. Along the way, pilgrims cleanse their souls and seek spiritual renewal as they reflect on life's profound questions. The rituals and practices associated with the Kumano pilgrimage, such as chanting, meditating, and participating in purifying ceremonies, foster a deep connection with nature and the divine.

Indeed, the sacred sites and spiritual journeys in Japanese mythology offer a glimpse into the rich tapestry of beliefs, traditions, and cultural heritage that define the Japanese people. The pilgrimage to these hallowed grounds serves as a conduit for spiritual growth and enlightenment. Whether it be the enchanting allure of Ise Jingu, the awe-inspiring presence of Mount Fuji, the mystical essence of Okinoshima, or the transformative power of Kumano, these sacred sites invite us to embark on a profound inward journey.

Each visit to these sacred sites becomes an opportunity to reconnect with the divine, transcend the boundaries of mortal existence, and tap into the vast reservoir of wisdom and spirituality that Japanese mythology embodies. The spiritual pilgrimages that unfold within these chapters of Japanese myth allow us to immerse ourselves in a world where the sacred merges with the mortal, and history, legend, and faith intertwine.

Ise Grand Shrine: The Home of Amaterasu

"Behold, the sanctuary of the sun goddess herself, Amaterasu," whispered the old priest, his voice barely audible amidst the surrounding sacred silence. The ancient trees surrounding the Ise Grand Shrine seemed to echo his words, as if emphasizing their importance. I stood in awe, mesmerized by the spiritual energy emanating from the shrine, feeling a connection to a world beyond my own comprehension.

In the heart of Mie Prefecture, Japan, lies the magnificent Ise Grand Shrine, a place revered by not only the Japanese people but also those who seek spiritual enlightenment from every corner of the globe. It is here that the spirit of Amaterasu, the goddess of the sun and the universe, resides in her earthly abode. The shrine holds an immense cultural and historical significance, rooted deep in the hearts of the Japanese people, reflecting a testament to their faith and reverence for ancient traditions.

The origins of the Ise Grand Shrine can be traced back over a millennium, to a time when Japan firmly believed in its indigenous Shinto religion. The shrine is dedicated to Amaterasu Omikami, considered to be the supreme deity in Shintoism and the ancestral deity of the Imperial family. As such, the Ise Grand Shrine is a symbol of the unity between the divine and the Japanese people.

The journey to the Ise Grand Shrine is not merely a physical one but also a journey of the spirit. Pilgrims from all walks of life travel great distances to experience the divine energy that permeates every inch of this sacred place. As I made my way through the torii gates, each step felt like a step closer to understanding the mysteries of the universe itself.

Despite its immense importance, the Ise Grand Shrine is one of the most enigmatic shrines in Japan. Its grandeur lies not in grand architecture or ostentatious displays but in its sublime simplicity and harmonious integration with the surrounding landscape. The shrine follows the architectural style of Shinmei-zukuri, characterized by its thatched roofs and wooden pillars. The structures are carefully preserved and rebuilt every 20 years, in accordance with the ancient Shinto belief in the cycle of life and renewal.

I found myself standing before the most sacred structure in the complex, the Naiku or Inner Shrine. Guarded by tall evergreen trees, it exudes an aura of tranquility and serenity. Upon entering, I was immediately captivated by the pure, spiritual atmosphere that enveloped me. The inner courtyard, Taka-ike, features a natural spring called the Isuzu River, renowned for its supposed purifying powers. Pilgrims gather here to purify themselves before embarking on their spiritual journey within the shrine.

As I took a moment to drink water from the Isuzu River, I reflected on the significance of purification in Shintoism. Water, in its purest form, symbolizes the cleansing of both body and soul. This act of purification brings the pilgrim closer to the divine, allowing for a deep spiritual connection with the universe and a sense of inner peace.

Moving further into the shrine, I approached the most revered location within the Naiku: the main sanctuary, commonly referred to as the Shin-den. Accessible only to the priests, this sacred dwelling is the home of Amaterasu herself. As I gazed at the solemn wooden structure, I couldn't help but feel a sense of awe and reverence. The presence of the goddess, though intangible, was undeniably alive within these sacred walls.

In addition to the Naiku, the complex also houses the Geku or Outer Shrine, where the goddess Toyouke, the deity of agriculture and industry, is enshrined. The Geku emphasizes the vital role of agriculture in Japanese society, paying homage to the divine power that sustains and nourishes the land and its people. The Geku, with its lush greenery and vibrant atmosphere, invites visitors to experience the harmonious relationship between humans and nature.

Exploring the Ise Grand Shrine, one cannot help but be overwhelmed by the sheer spiritual potency that emanates from this sacred place. Amidst the beauty of the natural surroundings, one can sense a delicate balance between tradition and progress, creating a harmonious coexistence between the ancient customs and the modern world.

As day turned to night, I observed the shrine under a different light. The soft glow of lanterns illuminated the walkways, casting an ethereal spell over the entire complex. The atmosphere was captivating, and it felt as if time itself had come to a standstill. I found solace in these waning hours, contemplating the profound connection between the human spirit and the divine.

Beyond its spiritual significance, the Ise Grand Shrine holds a deeper cultural symbolism. It serves as a reminder of the strength and resilience of the Japanese people throughout history. Despite the ravages of time, the shrine has persevered, its rituals and traditions passed down through generations. It stands as a testament to the unwavering commitment of the Japanese people to honor and preserve their ancestral heritage.

As I reluctantly bid farewell to the Ise Grand Shrine, my heart was filled with a profound sense of gratitude. The experience had touched my soul in ways I could never fully articulate. It had awakened within me a greater appreciation for the beauty of nature, the power of tradition, and the eternal mysteries of the divine.

I left the sacred grounds of the Ise Grand Shrine with a renewed spirit, carrying the eternal flame of faith and enlightenment in my heart. The shrine remains etched in my memory, an everlasting reminder of the profound connection between humans and the divine. And as I venture forth in life, I carry with me the lessons learned within its hallowed walls, forever grateful for the spiritual sanctuary that is the Ise Grand Shrine: the home of Amaterasu.

Mt. Fuji: The Sleeping Kami of the Land

As the sun rises in the Land of the Rising Sun, casting its golden glow on the surrounding landscapes, one majestic peak stands tall and proud, seemingly watching over the entire land. This iconic symbol, regarded as the sacred heart of Japan, is none other than Mount Fuji, a dormant volcano that has captivated hearts and minds for centuries.

At a staggering height of 3,776 meters (12,389 feet), Mount Fuji, or Fujisan as it is affectionately called by the locals, dominates the horizon and captures the imagination of all who behold it. Its perfectly conical shape, painted in snow during winter, and lush green during summer, has inspired countless artists, poets, and writers throughout history. But beyond its physical grandeur, there is a deeper, mystical significance that has made Mount Fuji a revered spiritual entity in Japanese culture.

The word "kami" in Japanese translates to "god" or "divine being." Despite Japan being a country where Shintoism, Buddhism, and other religious beliefs coexist harmoniously, the kami of Mount Fuji holds a special place in the hearts of the Japanese people. It is believed that the mountain itself is a guardian deity, a sleeping kami whose essence pervades the land.

Shrouded in a rich tapestry of myths and legends, Mount Fuji has been an integral part of Japanese folklore for centuries. According to one popular tale, the mountain was formed from the tears of a weeping goddess who had been separated from her heavenly lover. Despondent, she wept so much that her tears formed the majestic peak we see today. This myth not only gives a romantic explanation for the mountain's inception but also depicts the emotional connection between the people and the land they inhabit.

The spiritual significance of Mount Fuji extends beyond mythology, resonating with the practice of asceticism and meditation among Buddhist monks. For centuries, these secluded sanctuaries have dotted the mountain's base and slopes, attracting those who seek enlightenment and spiritual awakening. The strenuous pilgrimage to the summit, known as the Fuji-ko, has been undertaken by many, with each step considered a step towards self-discovery and purification.

To understand the profound spiritual connection between the people and Mount Fuji, you must delve into the realm of Shintoism, Japan's indigenous religion. Shinto followers believe that kami inhabit natural features such as mountains, rivers, and trees, embodying the essence of the divine within them. Thus, Mount Fuji becomes a resting place for the sleeping kami, a sacred space where the earthly and heavenly realms intertwine.

The spiritual magnetism of Mount Fuji extends beyond the realm of religion and mythology. The mountain's majesty has been a constant source of artistic inspiration throughout history. From ancient woodblock prints to contemporary photographs, artists have sought to capture the mountain's ethereal beauty, believing that they are glimpsing the very essence of the divine.

Mount Fuji's fame transcends geographical boundaries and calls to the hearts of people worldwide. Its presence has even inspired the Fuji Declaration, a global charter for peace and well-being, conceived at the Fuji Sanctuary located at the foot of the mountain. This declaration seeks to awaken the inherent divinity within every human being, encouraging them to protect the earth and forge a universal bond of shared responsibility.

As one gazes upon Mount Fuji, it is impossible not to be overwhelmed by its grandeur and the spiritual weight it carries. It stands as a reminder of the eternal connection between humanity and the land in which it resides. It urges us to reevaluate our relationship with nature and recognize the intrinsic divinity within ourselves and everything around us.

While this chapter merely scratches the surface of Mount Fuji's significance, it is fitting to leave you with a profound appreciation for the sacred beauty of this sleeping kami. As the mountains stand silent and steadfast, they embody the hopes, dreams, and aspirations of generations past, present, and future. Let us all strive to protect and honor this sacred existence, for in doing so, we may find ourselves awakening the dormant divinity within our own souls.

Kinkaku-ji and the Golden Whispers of the Past

As the morning sun began to cast its warm glow upon the ancient city of Kyoto, a gentle breeze swirled through the tranquil gardens of Kinkaku-ji, whispering tales of a bygone era. Nestled amidst a lush landscape, the renowned Golden Pavilion stood proudly, its shimmering surface reflecting the serenity that permeated this hallowed ground. Intriguing stories unfolded within these sacred grounds, capturing the hearts of those fortunate enough to explore its mysteries.

Kinkaku-ji, also known as the Temple of the Golden Pavilion, was not just an architectural marvel but a testament to the rich history and culture of Japan. Its origins could be traced back to the late 14th century, when it served as a retreat for the influential shogun Ashikaga Yoshimitsu. The temple was designed to embody the opulence and grandeur of the ruling class, with its top two floors adorned entirely in gold leaf.

As our journey into the past commences, let us acquaint ourselves with the vivid characters that animated the temple's history. At the heart of this tale lies Ashikaga Yoshimitsu, a man whose vision far surpassed the confines of his time. Yoshimitsu, a man of refined taste and unyielding ambition, desired to construct a place that would leave an indelible mark on Kyoto's landscape.

Among his numerous accomplishments, Yoshimitsu commissioned the construction of his retirement villa, which would later become

the Golden Pavilion. His ambition was to create a resplendent
structure that would evoke the majesty of paradise on earth. To
bring his vision to life, Yoshimitsu enlisted the finest architects and
artisans of the era, each contributing their unique expertise to the
unfolding masterpiece. The Golden Pavilion stood proudly at the
edge of a tranquil pond, carefully positioned to mirror its radiant
splendor. A testament to the brilliance of Japanese Zen Buddhism,
Kinkaku-ji harmoniously integrated natural elements and spiritual
symbolism. The lower floor, known as the Chamber of Dharma
Waters, represented the earthly realm, showcasing immaculate
architecture and delicate gardens. Here, visitors could lose
themselves in the tranquil melodies flowing from the temple's
surroundings. Curiosity piqued, we embark on our exploration,
stepping into the realm of the transcendent. Adjacent to the Chamber
of Dharma Waters, the middle floor emerged in breathtaking glory—
its golden facade glimmering in the soft light. Aptly named the Tower
of Sound Waves, this level housed a shrine where Buddhist disciples
gathered for meditation. The intricate attention to architectural
detail painted a vivid testament to Yoshimitsu's devotion to his
spiritual journey. However, the pinnacle of Kinkaku-ji awaited us
atop the temple—an enchanting culmination of Yoshimitsu's dreams.
The upper floor, known as the Cupola of the Ultimate, was a beacon
of gold, radiating ethereal beauty far and wide. Its pinnacle, adorned
with a majestic phoenix sculpture, seemed to touch the heavens
themselves. In this space, Yoshimitsu sought transcendence,
pursuing a spiritual realm where mortals could barely tread.
As daylight bathed the Golden Pavilion, casting shadows upon its

golden exterior, a sense of awe enveloped those who walked its hallowed grounds. It was a living testament to the ebb and flow of history, a haven where the whispering voices of the past could still be heard. Each step taken carried with it the echoes of ancient rituals, the footsteps of visitors long gone, and the whispers of profound conversations held beneath its glistening roof.

However, no chapter in history stands immune to the ravages of time. A cloud of melancholy loomed over Kinkaku-ji when, in 1950, a catastrophic fire reduced the Golden Pavilion to ashes. The temple's destruction reverberated throughout Japan, leaving an indelible mark on the collective memory of its people. Yet, like a phoenix rising from its own ashes, the spirit of Kinkaku-ji remained unbroken. The Japanese community rallied together, pledging their support to rebuild the temple that captured their hearts.

Navigating through the shadows of the temple's past, we transition into the present—a world where Kinkaku-ji stands once again, resurrected with unwavering determination. The Golden Pavilion, a testament to human resilience, now thrives as a UNESCO World Heritage site, drawing countless visitors from around the globe. Travelers flock to this oasis of tranquility, seeking solace in the temple's golden embrace. As we bid farewell to the resplendent Kinkaku-ji, let us reflect upon the messages whispered by its gleaming façade. The Golden Pavilion transcends time, serving as a gateway into the rich heritage and profound spiritualism of Japan. It is a poignant reminder of the impermanence of all things, as well as a celebration of the resilience of the human spirit.

Itsukushima Shrine: Where the Divine and Mortal Realms Meet

Nestled serenely on the island of Miyajima in Japan, surrounded by the scenic beauty of the Seto Inland Sea, lies a place where the ethereal and earthly worlds embrace in perfect harmony—the Itsukushima Shrine. This captivating shrine has enchanted visitors for centuries, with its awe-inspiring architecture, spiritual significance, and a unique feature that sets it apart from any other place of worship in the world—the famous "floating" Torii gate. Join me on a remarkable journey through history and spirituality as we dive into the enchanting world of the Itsukushima Shrine.

The Itsukushima Shrine, also known as Itsukushima-jinja, is a Shinto shrine dedicated to the three daughters of the Shinto deity Susano-o no Mikoto and constructed during the 6th century. Revered as a sacred and divine abode, this shrine embodies the essence of Shinto beliefs and practices, establishing a profound connection between the supernatural realm and the terrestrial sphere.

As I approached the entrance of the shrine, a sense of tranquility enveloped my being, brought on by the scent of ancient wood, wafting from the impressive vermillion corridors and towering pillars. The rhythmic hum of distant waves mingled with the melodies of birds, creating an ethereal symphony that resonated deep within my soul. It was as if the very essence of nature was embracing me, inviting me to explore this spiritual haven.

Walking along the meticulously crafted wooden planks, my gaze fixated on the vermilion-lacquered buildings, accentuated by elegant and elaborate architectural details. Intricate carvings of mythical creatures, divine deities, and sacred symbols adorned the structures, breathing life into an otherwise static timber frame. With each step I took, I couldn't help but marvel at the level of craftsmanship displayed, as if the hands of skilled artisans from generations past had left an indelible mark on every fiber of this place.

Reaching the heart of the shrine, I encountered the grandest spectacle—the majestic floating Torii gate. Rising proudly from the cobalt sea, this vibrant vermilion gate stood as a testament to the power of human ingenuity and spiritual transcendence. Built on wooden pilings, the gate appears to defy gravity, suspended above the water's surface during high tide, lending an otherworldly allure to the shrine.
This unique architectural marvel is no mere coincidence but a result of a deep understanding of the natural forces that govern the region. The strategic positioning of the Torii gate was reminiscent of the ancient Japanese belief that the boundary between the divine and mortal realms is a fluid one—a domain that blurs during moments of spiritual significance. Silhouetted against the backdrop of crisp blue skies or embraced by the waters during high tide, the floating Torii reminded me of the ephemeral nature of existence—a delicate dance

between the tangible and the intangible.

Stepping through the Torii gate, I found myself immersed in a realm that transcended time and mortal limitations. The inner sanctum of the shrine revealed an aura of sacredness and mystique, transporting me to a different plane of existence. The rhythmic chants of Shinto prayers reverberated through the air, accompanied by the sound of bells chiming softly in the distance. Vibrant offerings of colorful banners, sacred stones, and meticulously folded origami creations adorned the altar, symbolizing a profound reverence for the divine.

As I explored the various halls and pagodas within the shrine's complex, I uncovered a tapestry of stories interwoven with ancient rituals and legends. The Haiden, or prayer hall, served as a gathering place for devotees to offer their prayers to the kami—a pantheon of deities revered in Shintoism. The hushed whispers of contemplation filled the air, creating an atmosphere charged with faith and devotion.

Adjacent to the shrine, a sacred theatre known as Noh Stage stood as a testament to the long-held tradition of performing captivating mythical plays. Noh, a classical Japanese art form, often portrayed tales of legendary heroes and gods, perpetuating cultural heritage and promoting a deeper understanding of the divine realm. The intricately crafted masks and elaborate costumes added an element of mystique and elegance to these performances, captivating the audience and transporting them into the realm of myth and folklore. Beyond its rich cultural and spiritual significance, the Itsukushima Shrine also played a vital role in the local community's daily life, acting as a hub for various social and ceremonial events. Festivals such as the Miyajima Water Fireworks Festival and the Kangensai Music Festival brought together people from all walks of life, forging bonds and celebrating the shared cultural heritage of the inhabitants of Miyajima Island.

As the sun dipped below the horizon, casting an amber glow upon the waters surrounding the shrine, I couldn't help but reflect on the momentous journey I had experienced within these hallowed grounds. Itsukushima Shrine, with its unparalleled natural beauty and spiritual significance, serves as a timeless testament to the inherent human desire to connect with the divine. It is a place where heaven and earth intertwine, inviting us to embrace the infinite possibilities that lie beyond the realm of the known.

As I turned to leave the Itsukushima Shrine, a profound sense of gratitude washed over me—gratitude for the architects and artisans who crafted this spiritual haven, gratitude for the natural forces that shaped its existence, and gratitude for the countless individuals who have nurtured and preserved its sacred essence throughout the ages. Exiting through the floating Torii gate, I couldn't help but carry with me a piece of the divine connection that eternally resides within this mystical sanctuary.

The Itsukushima Shrine—an ethereal masterpiece, evoking a sense of reverence and awe within all who venture into its sanctuary. May its sacred aura continue to enchant and inspire generations to come, bridging the gap between the divine and the mortal realms, guiding us towards a profound understanding of our place in the cosmos.

CHAPTER 5: FESTIVALS AND RITUALS: CELEBRATING THE KAMI

In the realm of Shinto, the indigenous religion of Japan, festivals and rituals play a vital role in connecting with and honoring the kami, the divine spirits believed to inhabit various aspects of nature. Spanning from extravagant festivals attended by thousands to intimate household rituals, these celebrations bring communities closer together while fostering a deep reverence for the mystical forces that shape their lives. This chapter delves into the rich tapestry of Shinto festivals and rituals, exploring their origins, significance, and the various forms they take across the archipelago.

Section 1: Roots of Shinto Festivals

1.1 Legends and Origins:

To comprehend the significance of Shinto festivals, one must delve into the folklore and legends that provide their foundation. Many festivals can trace their roots back to tales of the kami, such as Amaterasu, the sun goddess, who withdrew to a cave and created darkness that only ended when the other gods performed a joyous dance outside. These legends often serve as the basis for the rituals enacted during festivals, as communities strive to recreate the sacred actions of their mythological ancestors.

1.2 Agricultural Beginnings:

Agriculture has been the backbone of Japanese society for centuries, and many festivals center around the seasons and the blessings of abundant harvests. These agricultural roots lie deep within the history of Japan, connecting communities to their land and reinforcing their dependence on the kami for fertile fields. Observing the traditions associated with planting, tending, and reaping, these festivals ensure a harmonious relationship with the land while expressing gratitude for its abundance.

Section 2: Major Shinto Festivals

2.1 Setsubun Mamemaki: Banishing Evil Spirits:

Setsubun Mamemaki, held each year on February 3rd, marks the transition from winter to spring and symbolizes casting out evil spirits from homes and communities. During this festival, people throw roasted soybeans (mame) while shouting, "Oni wa soto! Fuku wa uchi!" (Demons out, good fortune in!). This boisterous tradition reflects the vibrant and jovial nature of Shinto festivals and is believed to ward off misfortune while inviting prosperity for the year ahead.

2.2 Gion Matsuri: Celebrating Kyoto's Guardian Deity:

Among the grandest of all Shinto festivals, Gion Matsuri, held in Kyoto throughout July, honors the guardian deity of the city—Yasaka

Shrine. The event encompasses various rituals, culminating in the Yamaboko Junko, a dazzling parade of floats through the city streets. Gion Matsuri captures the essence of traditional Japanese culture, attracting millions of visitors each year who witness the majestic spectacle while paying homage to Kyoto's divine protector.

2.3 Obon: Honoring Ancestors' Spirits:

Obon, an odyssey celebrated in midsummer, is a deeply rooted festival where people visit ancestral graves, illuminate lanterns, and dance the Bon Odori. This event serves as a remembrance of deceased family members, welcoming their spirits back to the realm of the living. The comforting tradition of Obon reinforces familial ties, fostering a sense of continuity and an appreciation for the cyclical nature of life and death.

Section 3: Rituals and Ceremonies

3.1 Modern Shinto Weddings:

Weddings, an essential milestone for many, take on a distinct Shinto flavor in Japan. These ceremonies blend ancient rituals, such as the exchanging of nuptial cups called san-san-kudo, with contemporary touches. The bride and groom are purified before the kami, signifying their entrance into a sacred union blessed by the divine. Shinto weddings illustrate the timeless connection between spirituality, tradition, and family in Japanese society.

3.2 Hatsumode: Welcoming the New Year:

Each year, millions of Japanese flock to Shinto shrines for

Hatsumode, the first visit of the year, to pay respect to the kami and seek divine blessings for the year ahead. Visitors cleanse themselves at the temizuya, a water pavilion, before offering prayers and purchasing omamori, amulets believed to bring good fortune and protection. Hatsumode serves as a spiritual reset, instilling hope and optimism in hearts after bidding farewell to the old year.

3.3 Kagura Dance Rituals:

Kagura, an ancient dance ritual performed at Shinto shrines, showcases the power and beauty of movement. Dancers, adorned in traditional costumes, interpret myths and legends through intricate choreography, accompanied by ethereal music. These performances function as a conduit for the kami, inviting their presence while inviting spectators to immerse themselves in the magical world of Shinto mythology.

As we have explored within this chapter, the festivities and rituals of Shinto reflect the deep-rooted spiritual connection between the Japanese people and the kami. Whether honoring the changing seasons, paying tribute to ancestral spirits, or celebrating life's milestones, these events are a testament to the vibrant tradition and the sense of community fostered by Shinto. By partaking in these rich and diverse ceremonies, individuals transcend everyday life, immersing themselves in the transcendent realm of the kami.

Tanabata: The Star-Crossed Lovers of Mythology

In the vast realm of mythology, countless tales of love and tragedy have been passed down through generations. These captivating stories have provided solace, inspiration, and moral lessons to people across different cultures. Among these narratives, the tale of Tanabata reigns as one of the most poignant and enduring love stories in Japanese folklore. Rooted in the delicate threads of love and heartache, Tanabata weaves a tale of longing, sacrifice, and the unbreakable bond between two celestial beings. Journey with us as we explore the intriguing world of Tanabata, in the land of the rising sun.

Section 1: Origins

Tanabata, also known as the Star Festival, finds its origins in Chinese mythology before making its way to Japan, where it has become an integral part of Japanese culture, celebrated every year on the 7th day of the 7th lunar month. The story behind this festival revolves around two lovers, Vega and Altair, who are separated by the Celestial River, or Amanogawa – a metaphorical representation of the Milky Way.

Section 2: The Celestial Weaver and the Cowherd

The protagonist of our tale, Princess Orihime, is the Celestial Weaver, symbolizing the star Vega. Orihime was the daughter of Tentei, the

Sky King, and was known for being exceptionally skilled at weaving. Legend has it that Orihime spent her days weaving magnificent garments to adorn the gods and celestial beings. However, her relentless dedication to her craft left her isolated and lonely, yearning for companionship.

On the other side of the Celestial River resided Hikoboshi, the Cowherd, who represents the star Altair. Hikoboshi was a diligent and hardworking soul, tending to his cattle with utmost care and love. Living a tranquil existence amidst nature, he too longed for a companion.

Section 3: Love Blossoms

Moved by the longing in their hearts, Tentei arranged for the paths of Orihime and Hikoboshi to cross. Their first encounter under a clear night sky intensified their feelings of loneliness, and a connection was instantly forged. Their shared emotions developed into a profound love, filling the void in their hearts.

As their love blossomed, Orihime's weaving suffered, and Hikoboshi's cattle were neglected. Observing this imbalance, Tentei grew concerned and decided to intervene. He consented to their union, allowing the two star-crossed lovers to be married, much to their joy and satisfaction.

Section 4: Separation and Grief

Following their union, Orihime and Hikoboshi were inseparable.

Their days were filled with laughter, love, and companionship. However, as days turned into months, their happiness was tainted by their neglect of their respective duties. The once vibrant patterns created by Orihime's loom began to diminish, and Hikoboshi's cattle began to wander aimlessly, unattended.

Concerned with the sudden decline in productivity within the celestial realm, Tentei decided to take action. He declared that Orihime and Hikoboshi could no longer be together. The ruling separated the lovers, condemning them to reside on opposite sides of the Celestial River. The Milky Way was transformed into an impassable barrier, leaving the two lovers gazing upon each other with a profound sadness that engulfed their souls.

Section 5: The Magpie Bridge and Tanabata Festival
Moved by the heartfelt pain experienced by Orihime and Hikoboshi, the magpies, known for their cleverness, empathy, and ability to bridge gaps, devised a plan. They proposed building a bridge of magpie wings that would span the Celestial River for a single day each year. This bridge would allow Orihime and Hikoboshi to reunite and cherish their love, even if for a short time.

To commemorate this reunion, the Tanabata Festival was born. Celebrated annually on the 7th day of the 7th lunar month, the festival invites people to make their wishes and write them on colorful strips of paper known as tanzaku. These tanzaku are then tied to bamboo branches, representing the magpie bridge, in hopes that their prayers will be granted by the celestial realms.

Section 6: Contemporary Significance

Over time, the tale of Tanabata has evolved into a cultural phenomenon celebrated across Japan. Schools, communities, and even entire cities come alive with vibrant decorations, colorful parades, and traditional attire. People often engage in various traditional activities such as writing their wishes on tanzaku, participating in traditional dances, and enjoying the ethereal beauty of countless paper lanterns.

Tanabata has also been embraced beyond Japan's borders and has made its way into global consciousness, captivating individuals with its emotional depth and universal themes of love and longing. Each year, people from all walks of life gather under a starlit sky, contemplating the transcendent power of love and the resilience of the human spirit.

Although Tanabata is an ancient Japanese myth, its story resonates with individuals today as it did centuries ago. The saga of Princess Orihime and Hikoboshi serves as a captivating reminder that even in the face of separation and adversity, love can endure and bridge seemingly insurmountable gaps. As we continue to celebrate the Tanabata Festival, let us cherish this timeless tale and remember that love holds the power to ignite our spirits, connect our souls, and overcome all obstacles.

Obon: Honoring the Spirits of Ancestors

In the heart of Japan's spiritual calendar lies a sacred festival called Obon, a time when ancestral spirits return to this earthly realm for a joyous reunion with their loved ones. This extraordinary celebration not only showcases the deep reverence that the Japanese have for their ancestors but also offers a glimpse into the rich tapestry of folklore, tradition, and cultural expression that is woven into the fabric of this ancient nation. In this chapter, we delve into the captivating world of Obon, exploring its history, practices, and the profound significance it holds for the people of Japan.

Origins and Historical Background

Obon can be traced back over 500 years ago to the era known as Muromachi, a period marked by regional unrest and social upheaval in Japan. During this time, it was believed that the spirits of the deceased returned to the earthly realm for a brief visit. However, it was not until the Edo period (1603-1868) that Obon took the form that we recognize today.

Legend has it that a Buddhist monk named Mokuren was deeply concerned about the suffering of his deceased mother's spirit. He sought the guidance of the Buddha, who advised him to perform a ritual over a period of fifteen days to comfort her soul. Following the

Buddha's instructions, Mokuren invited fellow monks to join him in chanting sutras to liberate ancestral spirits trapped in the realm between life and death. This marked the beginning of what would later evolve into Obon.

The Observance of Obon

Obon is observed in most regions of Japan, predominantly during the month of August. However, certain areas, such as the northern regions of Tohoku, adhere to the older lunar calendar, celebrating Obon in July. The festival is a time when families come together to pay homage to their ancestors, offering prayers, performing rituals, and engaging in festivities that honor the spirits.

One of the most visually striking features of Obon is the lighting of bonfires and lanterns. These symbolize a guiding light to help spirits locate their families amidst the earthly realm. The bonfires, known as "mukaebi," are lit on the first day of Obon to welcome the spirits, while the lanterns, called "toro nagashi," are set afloat on rivers and seas on the final day, guiding the spirits on their journey back to the otherworldly realm.

Customs and Practices of Obon

Obon is not just a religious observance; it is a time for communities to come together and celebrate the interconnectedness of life and death. Throughout the festival, various customs and practices are followed, each with its own unique significance.

One of the most prominent customs of Obon is the construction of "Obon altars" in homes. These altars, adorned with offerings of food, water, and flowers, serve as a sacred space where families gather to honor and remember their ancestors. It is believed that the spirits of the departed return to the physical world during Obon, and the altar acts as a tangible representation of their presence.

Another important practice during Obon is "mukaebi dances." These traditional dances, performed in a circular formation, are undertaken to welcome ancestral spirits. Each region and community may have its own unique style of dance, but the principle remains the same - to honor and celebrate the spirits that have returned.

Food plays a central role during Obon as well. Families often prepare special meals, called "Obon dishes," that consist of the favorite foods of their ancestors. These meals are shared with the spirits, with the belief that they will nourish the souls and provide comfort during their visit. Water is also placed in small vessels to quench the thirst of the spirits, who have journeyed from the otherworldly realm to visit their loved ones.

Obon Festivities

Obon is not only about solemn ceremonies and rituals; it is also a time for celebration and enjoyment. Festivities during this time capture the vibrant essence of Japanese culture, combining music, dance, parades, and entertainment.

One of the most celebrated aspects of Obon across Japan is the Bon Odori, or Obon dance festival. Communities gather in open spaces, adorned in traditional attire, to dance to the rhythmic beats of taiko drums and joyous folk melodies. Men, women, and children of all ages come together to partake in this lively event, fostering a sense of community and unity.

In addition to the Bon Odori, many regions also hold lantern festivals known as "toro nagashi." This spectacular sight sees countless paper lanterns being released onto rivers, carrying with them the prayers of the living and guiding the spirits back to their otherworldly abode. The ethereal beauty of these lanterns, silently floating downstream, is a sight to behold and evokes a sense of peace and tranquility.

Obon holds a special place in the hearts of the Japanese people, embodying their reverence for ancestors, remembering loved ones, and embracing the cycle of life and death. Through its customs, rituals, and festivities, Obon serves as a bridge between the seen and unseen worlds, creating a profound connection that resonates with both spiritual seekers and cultural enthusiasts alike.

As the bonfires illuminate the night sky and lanterns dance upon the waters, Obon reminds us of the enduring bonds between the living and the departed. It invites us to reflect on the impermanence of life, the interconnectedness of all beings, and the importance of honoring those who came before us. Obon is not just a festival; it is a testament to the enduring power of love and remembrance, offering solace to our souls and guiding us on a path of meaningful existence.

Setsubun: The Ritualistic Ousting of Evil Spirits

Throughout history, various cultures and civilizations have developed their unique customs and rituals to ward off evil and celebrate the changing of seasons. In Japan, one such tradition is Setsubun, a vibrant festival observed annually on February 3rd. Setsubun, which translates to "seasonal division," is a time-honored event when Japanese people come together to drive away evil spirits and invite good luck and fortune into their lives. This chapter delves into the fascinating world of Setsubun, exploring its origins, practices, and enduring significance in contemporary Japan.

Origins of Setsubun

The roots of Setsubun can be traced back to ancient Chinese customs associated with the Lunar New Year. These early practices involved individuals throwing roasted soybeans, known as "mamemaki," to drive away malevolent spirits or "oni." This tradition was believed to bring good luck and prosperity for the coming year.

Over time, the ritual was incorporated into Shintoism, Japan's indigenous religion. Setsubun soon became associated with the changing of seasons, particularly the transition from winter to spring – a vital time marked by the renewal of life and the emergence of new possibilities. Through the centuries, Setsubun has evolved and assimilated elements from Buddhist and folk beliefs, making it a unique mix of customs and superstitions.

Preparation for Setsubun

The preparation for Setsubun begins well in advance, as households gear up to cleanse their living spaces and ensure a fresh start for the upcoming year. Families thoroughly clean their homes, known as "souji," removing any negative energy or "kegare," which is associated with misfortune. This purifying act is seen as a means of inviting positive spirits and blessings into the household.

In addition to cleansing, families adorn their homes with traditional Setsubun decorations, such as paper lanterns, lucky charms, and auspicious symbols like tiger heads and devil masks. These items are believed to protect against evil spirits and bring good fortune.

The Ritualistic Ousting of Evil Spirits

Setsubun officially begins at sundown on February 3rd, as families gather together to partake in the vibrant and joyous festivities. The central ritual of Setsubun involves the casting out of evil spirits, symbolized by the throwing of soybeans. This act, known as "mamemaki," is performed primarily by the head of the household facing the main entrance or towards a designated direction.

Accompanied by chants, the person throws roasted soybeans both inside and outside the house, yelling, "Oni wa soto! Fuku wa uchi!" meaning "Out with the demons, in with fortune!" According to tradition, the aim is to expel the evil spirits and prevent them from entering the home while simultaneously bringing in blessings and good luck.

During this ceremony, other family members enthusiastically shout and applaud, creating a lively and festive atmosphere. Young children, clad in playful devil or monster masks, often take great joy in assisting their parents with the mamemaki, fostering a sense of unity and participation.

Symbolism and Folk Beliefs

Setsubun is not only a fun event for families across Japan but is also imbued with symbolism and associated folk beliefs. The custom of throwing soybeans is deeply rooted in ancient superstitions, as soybeans are believed to possess spiritual power and the ability to purify the environment.

The choice of casting out evil spirits by throwing beans is linked to the belief that demons and supernatural creatures despise the smell of soybeans, therefore repelling them from the household. Additionally, it is believed that beans have the unique ability to absorb negative energy, making them an effective tool in driving away misfortune.

Alongside soybeans, other symbolic items are employed during mamemaki, including small bills, sweets, and even gold and silver items. People throw these objects into a crowd, further emphasizing the idea of spreading good fortune and prosperity amongst their loved ones and the community.

Setsubun Beyond the Home

While Setsubun is primarily observed in homes, its influence extends far beyond the domestic sphere. Temples and shrines across Japan hold special Setsubun ceremonies, attracting large congregations eager to participate in the age-old tradition. These public events often include performances, dances, and iconic rituals, amplifying the celebratory atmosphere.

One such iconic ritual is the "Mamemaki by Famous Celebrities," where famous personalities, entertainers, or sumo wrestlers participate in mamemaki events at temples, attracting vast crowds. These events give the public an opportunity to join in the festivities, seek blessings, and witness their favorite celebrities engaging in the traditional ritual.

Furthermore, schools and community organizations also organize Setsubun events, involving children in mamemaki and educating them about the cultural significance of the festival. By introducing Setsubun to the younger generation, Japan ensures the continued preservation and passing down of this cherished tradition.

Setsubun in Modern Times

As Japan has embraced modernity, Setsubun has adapted to contemporary society while holding on to its timeless essence. While traditions remain the same at their core, new practices and interpretations have arisen. One notable example is the emergence of themed mamemaki events, where people dress up as popular manga or anime characters while engaging in the ritual.

Moreover, Setsubun has also gained commercial popularity, with various products and treats being sold exclusively for the occasion. Setsubun-themed sweets, such as ehomaki (thick sushi rolls) and dorayaki (sweet pancake sandwiches), have become popular culinary staples during this festival. Companies use the charm and auspiciousness associated with Setsubun to market their products, further embedding this cultural celebration in modern society. Setsubun embodies Japan's deep-rooted respect for tradition and spiritual beliefs while celebrating the passage of time and the arrival of spring. Rooted in centuries-old customs and influenced by diverse cultural influences, this ritualistic festival remains a unique blend of folklore, Shintoism, and Buddhist practices.

Through the ritualistic ousting of evil spirits and the casting of soybeans, Setsubun continues to bring families closer together and foster a sense of community. The vibrant festivities, symbolic gestures, and optimistic beliefs associated with Setsubun serve as a reminder of the power and resilience of cultural traditions, ensuring that this remarkable festival endures for generations to come.

Gion Matsuri: A Festive Dance with the Gods

In the enchanting city of Kyoto, where ancient traditions blend seamlessly with modern innovations, lies a celebration of immense grandeur and cultural significance. This celebration is none other than the renowned Gion Matsuri, a vibrant festival that has been captivating the hearts and souls of the Japanese people for centuries. Originating during the Heian period (794-1185), Gion Matsuri is a spectacular and awe-inspiring event that pays homage to the gods, enthralls the masses with vibrant parades, and epitomizes the rich cultural heritage of Japan.

Gion Matsuri takes place throughout the month of July, with its highlight being the grand procession known as Yamahoko Junko, which takes place on the 17th and 24th of the month. This procession, often referred to as one of the most splendid in the world, features towering and ornate floats called "yamahoko." These magnificent structures, some towering up to 25 meters in height, are adorned with intricate designs, colorful tapestries, and elegant lanterns.

Preparations for the festival begin months in advance, with communities, temples, and neighborhoods all coming together to create and decorate these mammoth floats. The craftsmanship and attention to detail are simply astounding, with each float being meticulously constructed using traditional construction techniques that have been passed down through generations.

As the date of the Yamahoko Junko approaches, the excitement in Kyoto intensifies. The festival fills the air with an infectious energy, as locals dress in traditional yukatas, vibrant summer kimonos, eager to witness the spectacle unfold. Families and friends gather along the streets, claiming their spots to catch a glimpse of the procession and immerse themselves in this vivid cultural experience.

On the day of the parade, Kyoto's main avenue, Shijo Street, transforms into a bustling corridor of merriment. Crowds of both locals and tourists eagerly await the commencement of the procession, their curiosity piqued by the distant sounds of shrill flutes and thunderous drums gradually growing louder. The arrival of the Yamahoko floats marks the moment when time itself seems to stand still.

Each float represents a neighborhood or district within Kyoto, showcasing their unique heritage and individual artistic flair. As the giant floats maneuver the narrow streets, they exude an incredible sense of grace and balance, defying their colossal proportions. It is a testament to the skill and precision of the festival participants who steer these floats through the crowded streets, sometimes with mere inches to spare.

The Yamahoko Junko procession is not just a visual feast, but it also tantalizes the auditory senses with the accompanying musical performances. Traditional Japanese festival music echoes through the air, resonating with the rhythms of the parade. Shakuhachi flutes, taiko drums, and other ancient instruments fill the streets with melodies that whisk the onlookers into a world imbued with mystical charm.

Gion Matsuri is not solely about the spectacle of the Yamahoko floats; it is also an opportunity to glimpse into the spiritual essence of Japan. The festival, at its core, is a way of honoring the gods and seeking their divine blessings. As the floats weave their way through the city, they stop at various temples to perform rituals and offer prayers. These sacred moments allow both participants and spectators to feel connected to the divine forces that are believed to protect and guide the city.

One of the most significant religious aspects of Gion Matsuri is the Yoiyama. Held in the evenings leading up to the Yamahoko Junko, Yoiyama invites visitors to stroll along the streets of Kyoto's historic district, known as Gion. The streets come alive with numerous food stalls, traditional performances, and beautifully illuminated paper lanterns that cast a warm glow on the festivities. The atmosphere is enchanting, creating an otherworldly ambiance that captivates all those who wander through this magical tapestry.

However, Gion Matsuri is not just about large-scale processions and religious ceremonies; it also provides a platform for traditional performing arts to thrive. Throughout the festival, various traditional dance performances, known as "kagura," are held in shrines and temples across Kyoto. These spirited and graceful dances, dating back centuries, tell mythical tales and embody the spirit of ancient Japan. The performers, dressed in vibrant costumes, become vessels through which the gods communicate with the mortal realm, creating a mesmerizing experience that transports the audience to another era.

Gion Matsuri is a testament to the enduring spirit of the Japanese people and their reverence for their cultural heritage. It serves as a reminder that traditions, customs, and rituals can thrive in a modern world, bridging the gap between the past and present. The festival has weathered the test of time, transcending generations and political changes, and continues to draw millions of visitors from all corners of the globe who seek to uncover the essence of Japan.

As the grand Yamahoko Junko procession reaches its conclusion, and the floats are carefully disassembled and stored until the next year, the people of Kyoto reflect on the profound experience that Gion Matsuri provides. It is a time of gratitude, both for the gods who have protected the city and for the shared appreciation of culture and tradition.

Gion Matsuri is not simply a festival but an ode to the cultural legacy that unites the people of Kyoto and celebrates the diversity and depth of Japanese society. For the month of July, as the city takes on an ethereal aura, the gods and humans dance together in perfect harmony, creating a symphony of sights, sounds, and emotions that imprint themselves on the hearts of all those lucky enough to witness this mesmerizing event.

CHAPTER 6: MODERN INTERPRETATIONS AND CULTURAL INFLUENCES

Japanese mythology is deeply rooted in the country's history and culture. It has evolved over centuries, blending indigenous beliefs with imported ideas from China, Korea, and other neighboring regions. In this chapter, we will explore the modern interpretations and cultural influences on Japanese mythology. We will delve into how these myths have been interpreted and portrayed in various forms of art, literature, and popular culture, showcasing their significant impact on Japanese society.

1. The Role of Shinto and Buddhism in Japanese Mythology:
Shinto, the native religion of Japan, played a crucial role in shaping Japanese mythology. It focuses on the veneration of natural forces, spirits (known as kami), and divine beings. Kami are believed to dwell in natural elements like rocks, trees, rivers, and mountains. This emphasis on nature has influenced Japanese art and inspired many myths centered around nature and its harmonic relationship

with humans.

Buddhism, which arrived in Japan from China and Korea around the 6th century, brought with it a plethora of new deities, myths, and religious concepts. It introduced the idea of reincarnation and the cycle of life and death. Over time, Buddhism and Shinto gradually merged, giving birth to a syncretic religious system in Japan known as Shinbutsu-shūgō.

2. Mythological Themes in Japanese Literature:

Japanese mythology has greatly influenced classical Japanese literature, where myths were often used as metaphors and allegories. The oldest surviving Japanese written works, such as the Kojiki (Record of Ancient Matters) and the Nihon Shoki (Chronicles of Japan), contain numerous myths and legends that have shaped the literary landscape.

One of the most famous mythological stories found in Japanese literature is the Tale of the Bamboo Cutter (Taketori Monogatari). It tells the story of a girl named Kaguya-hime, who is found inside a bamboo stalk and raised by a bamboo cutter. This tale explores themes of love, loss, and the fleeting nature of human life, resonating deeply in the hearts of the Japanese people.

3. Mythology in Traditional Performing Arts:

Japanese mythology has also left a significant imprint on traditional performing arts. Noh theater, a classical form of musical drama, often incorporates mythological stories and characters. The plays typically revolve around themes of human suffering, redemption, and the quest for enlightenment.

Kabuki, another prominent form of traditional theater developed in the Edo period, also draws heavily from mythology. Kabuki plays often depict famous mythological figures such as Izanagi and Izanami, Amaterasu, and Susanoo, bringing these ancient stories to life on the stage with vibrant costumes, elaborate makeup, and dynamic performances.

4. Visual Art and Mythological Motifs:
Japanese mythology has provided a rich source of inspiration for visual artists throughout history. Traditional Japanese paintings, known as Yamato-e, often feature scenes from myths and legends. These artworks capture both the ethereal beauty of the celestial realms and the earthly struggles of humans.

In ukiyo-e, a popular art form during the Edo period, mythological themes are frequently depicted. Prints showcasing the adventures of the legendary hero, Yoshitsune, or the captivating landscapes of mythical creatures like dragons and phoenixes served as a form of entertainment for the masses.

5. Modern Interpretations in Manga and Anime:
Japanese mythology continues to thrive in contemporary forms of art and entertainment, particularly in manga and anime. These mediums

have reimagined ancient myths, introducing them to new audiences in exciting and innovative ways.

Popular manga series like "Naruto" draw heavily from Japanese folklore and mythology, featuring characters inspired by deities and mythical creatures. Anime films, such as Hayao Miyazaki's "Princess Mononoke," explore themes of environmentalism while incorporating Shinto influences and mythical creatures.

Modern interpretations and cultural influences have breathed new life into Japanese mythology, ensuring its preservation and relevance in contemporary society. The fusion of traditional beliefs with modern creativity has allowed these ancient myths to transcend time and geographical boundaries, captivating audiences both in Japan and around the world. By revisiting and reinterpreting these tales, we not only honor Japan's rich cultural heritage but also gain insights into the intricate tapestry of its mythology.

Anime and Manga: Mythology's New Canvas

Anime and manga have become a global phenomenon, captivating audiences with their unique storytelling and visually stunning artwork. From epic adventures to heartwrenching dramas, these Japanese creations have given birth to countless beloved characters and narratives. However, what many people may not realize is that beneath the surface of anime and manga lies a rich tapestry of mythology. Drawing from ancient legends and folklore, anime and manga creators have found a new canvas to explore and reimagine age-old stories in captivating and innovative ways. In this chapter, we will delve into the intricate relationship between anime, manga, and mythology, unraveling the threads that connect them and exploring how these mediums rejuvenate and reinvent ancient tales.

The Power of Mythology in Anime and Manga:

Mythology has a long and celebrated history, steeped in the traditions of countless cultures around the world. It serves as a vessel for universal truths, exploring human nature, morality, and the mysteries of the world. Anime and manga tap into the profound essence of mythology, breathing new life into these timeless narratives. By incorporating elements of mythology within their stories, creators instill a sense of familiarity while infusing them with fresh perspectives and interpretations. In doing so, they bring these myths to newer and broader audiences, shedding light on their enduring relevance in contemporary society.

Reimagining gods and goddesses:

One of the most striking aspects of anime and manga is how they reimagine gods and goddesses from various pantheons. These mythical beings, often depicted as larger-than-life figures controlling the forces of nature, are transformed into relatable characters grappling with personal struggles and desires. This humanization allows viewers and readers to forge emotional connections with these deities, prompting reflection on their own humanity in the process. Works such as "Noragami" and "High School DxD" give life to mythological beings like the Japanese gods and the Norse pantheon, weaving their stories into the fabric of contemporary settings and exploring their place in a modern world.

An interplay of Shinto and Folklore:

Shinto, the indigenous religion of Japan, plays a pivotal role in the mythological underpinnings of anime and manga. Deeply intertwined with the country's folklore and cultural identity, Shinto provides a rich tapestry of gods, spirits, and creatures that inspire countless creations. Anime like "Inuyasha" draws heavily from Japanese folklore, incorporating mythical creatures such as kitsunes, onis, and yōkai into its narrative. By blending these elements seamlessly, the medium pays homage to its cultural heritage while breathing new life into ancient tales.

Epic battles and the hero's journey:

Myths are often synonymous with grand battles and heroic quests, and anime and manga are no strangers to these epic adventures. Drawing inspiration from mythological heroes like Hercules and King Arthur, anime and manga protagonists embark on transformative journeys of self-discovery, facing insurmountable odds and triumphing over evil. The "Dragon Ball" series is a prime example, with its dynamic protagonist Goku embodying the archetypal hero on a quest to protect the Earth from powerful adversaries. Through these larger-than-life battles, anime and manga tap into the heroic spirit ingrained in mythology, inspiring viewers and readers to find their own strength and purpose.

A playground for supernatural creatures:

Mythology is a haven for supernatural beings – from vampires to demons and everything in between. Anime and manga offer creators an expansive playground to explore these creatures' stories, often pushing the boundaries of imagination. Works like "Bleach" and "Vampire Knight" delve into the world of vampires, presenting their own unique mythos and societal structures. By expanding upon the mythology surrounding these supernatural creatures, anime and manga captivate audiences with their imaginative world-building while simultaneously paying tribute to the myths that inspire them.

Folklore as a source of inspiration:

Beyond the realm of gods and supernatural beings, anime and manga also take inspiration from folklore, drawing from tales passed down through generations. These folk tales, rooted in cultural traditions and beliefs, offer creators an endless source of captivating narratives. Studio Ghibli's "Spirited Away" is a perfect example, weaving together elements from Japanese folklore to create a visually stunning and emotionally resonant tale. Through these adaptations, anime and manga honor their cultural roots and encourage viewers to explore and appreciate indigenous legends.

Within the vibrant worlds of anime and manga lies an intricate dance of mythology and creativity. By drawing from ancient legends, folklore, and cultural traditions, creators have forged a unique medium that breathes new life into timeless stories. Anime and manga offer a fresh canvas, infusing mythology with modern sensibilities, while preserving the core essence of these revered tales. As these mediums continue to evolve and captivate audiences worldwide, the intricate relationship with mythology ensures that the past and present coexist, inspiring generations to come.

Modern Literature: Whispers of the Old in the New

Japanese mythology is rich, diverse, and deeply ingrained in the cultural fabric of the country. Throughout history, these mythical tales have served as inspiration for poets, writers, and artists alike. In this chapter, we explore the realm of modern Japanese literature and how it weaves whispers of the old into the fabric of the new. By delving into the works of renowned authors and examining their use of mythology, we come to understand the symbiotic relationship between ancient folklore and contemporary narratives.

Embracing Tradition:

One of the striking aspects of modern Japanese literature is its profound respect for tradition. Many authors find solace in exploring and reimagining ancient myths, treating them as a wellspring of inspiration. By doing so, they ensure that these stories are not confined to history but continue to evolve, adapting to the needs and sensibilities of the present.

One contemporary writer who brilliantly channels the whispers of old myths is Haruki Murakami. In his highly acclaimed novel "Kafka on the Shore," Murakami intertwines the lives of two seemingly unrelated protagonists with elements of Japanese mythology. Through references to creatures like the "minotaur" and the use of parallel narrative structures, Murakami navigates the intersection of reality and fantasy, creating a modern-day myth infused with ancient symbolism.

Unearthing Legends:

Another way modern Japanese literature incorporates mythology is by unearthing hidden legends and crafting narratives around them. These stories, often obscure or forgotten, expose readers to lesser-known aspects of Japan's folklore. Authors adept at this skill resurrect legendary beings and events from the hoary past, offering fresh insights into a vast mythological landscape.

A prime example of this is Yukio Mishima's "The Sea of Fertility" tetralogy. The series spans four novels, each exploring a different era of Japanese history while simultaneously drawing on mythological motifs. Mishima seamlessly incorporates figures such as the "Eight-Forked Serpent" from Japanese creation myths, employing them as metaphors for the socio-political landscape. By intertwining historical events and myths, Mishima confronts Japan's turbulent past, laying bare its hidden secrets.

Myths as Metaphors:

Moving beyond overt references to folklore, contemporary Japanese authors skillfully employ myths as metaphors, infusing their works with profound symbolism and deeper meaning. By exploring the themes and characters found within mythology, these writers convey broader social, political, or philosophical concepts, resonating with readers on multiple levels.

A prominent author known for employing myths metaphorically is Banana Yoshimoto. In her novella "N.P.," Yoshimoto delves into the psyche of her characters through the lens of mythology. The story revolves around a translator unraveling the narrative of another writer, opening doors to a world where reality and imagination collide. Yoshimoto cleverly weaves together elements of ancient Shinto myths, using them as vehicles to explore complex themes of loss, longing, and redemption.

Reimagining Folklore:

While some authors hold tightly to the roots of tradition, others choose to venture into bold territory, daring to reinterpret and revitalize ancient tales. These reimagined myths traverse different time periods, genres, or settings, making the narratives both engaging and relatable to contemporary audiences.

A compelling example of mythological reimagining can be found in Kij Johnson's "The Fox Woman." Drawing inspiration from the Japanese Kitsune folklore, Johnson crafts a tantalizing tale set in medieval Japan. This meticulously researched work explores themes of transformation, desire, and the boundaries between human and animal. By infusing the story with sensual imagery and lyrical prose, Johnson breathes new life into an age-old myth, captivating readers with her fresh interpretation.

Modern Japanese literature is alive with whispers of ancient mythology. Through the works of authors like Haruki Murakami, Yukio Mishima, Banana Yoshimoto, and Kij Johnson, we witness a delicate dance between tradition and innovation. The stories crafted by these talented individuals bridge the gap between past and present, inviting readers to explore the enduring power of myth. As literature continues to evolve, it is imperative that we remember the intrinsic value of these age-old tales, for they hold our collective memories, mysteries, and dreams within their ethereal grasp.

Cinema: The Silver Screen's Homage to the Japanese Gods

Cinema is a mesmerizing art form that has the power to transport its viewers to new worlds, unravel intricate stories, and evoke a myriad of emotions. While the medium itself is a magnificent creation of human ingenuity, its roots can be traced back to ancient Japan, where the timeless myths and legends of gods and goddesses have fueled the imaginations of filmmakers around the globe. In this chapter, we explore how the silver screen pays homage to the enigmatic and awe-inspiring Japanese deities, infusing their divine essence into modern storytelling.

The Gods and Their Influence:

Japanese mythology boasts a rich tapestry of deities, each with their own unique traits and captivating tales. Among them, some have particularly resonated with filmmakers, inspiring them to weave their stories around these godly figures. One such example is Amaterasu, the Sun Goddess and the central figure of the Shinto religion. Known for her radiant beauty and divine power, Amaterasu has served as an embodiment of courage, hope, and sacrifice on the silver screen. Her presence in films often symbolizes the triumph of good over evil, and her character radiates a celestial charm that captivates audiences worldwide.

Another deity that has left an indelible mark on cinema is Susanoo, the tempestuous God of Storms and Sea. Known for his impulsive nature, Susanoo has inspired filmmakers to craft tales of tumultuous emotions and epic battles. Depicting his wrath through the forces of nature unleashed on-screen, directors have harnessed the awe-inspiring power of Susanoo to create visually stunning sequences that leave audiences breathless. From swirling tornadoes to raging tsunamis, these scenes are a testament to the god's volatile nature and the immense creative potential that his myth offers.

Furthermore, the enchanting goddess of love, beauty, and healing, Amaterasu's granddaughter, has made her presence felt in the realm of cinema as well. Benten, often depicted with a biwa (a traditional Japanese lute) and accompanied by a retinue of white snakes, exudes a serene aura that has captivated filmmakers. Her tranquil yet alluring nature has inspired graceful characters who navigate the complexities of love, desire, and self-discovery. The inclusion of Benten in cinematic narratives often adds a touch of mystique and elegance, enriching the tapestry of storytelling.

Japanese Gods Meet Animation:

The influence of Japanese mythology extends beyond live-action cinema, spreading its wings into the world of animation. In this realm, filmmakers have a unique opportunity to breathe life into the gods and goddesses, blending their magical essence with stunning visuals. Studio Ghibli, synonymous with extraordinary animated masterpieces, has explored this realm extensively. One of their notable films, "Princess Mononoke," intertwines human and divine conflicts, elegantly showcasing the clash between gods and mortals. The film's protagonist, Ashitaka, tangled in a complex web of divine intervention, embodies the delicate balance between humans and the gods they unknowingly provoke.

Similarly, the awe-inspiring work of Hayao Miyazaki, one of the greatest animation directors of our time, embodies the divine through the spirited character of Haku in "Spirited Away." With a captivating backstory rooted in ancient folklore, Haku transforms into a dragon, symbolizing a tantalizing blend of human and godly traits. Miyazaki's immaculate animation beautifully captures the essence of these divine creatures, infusing them with ethereal qualities that linger long after the film ends.

Modern Adaptations and Homages:

While traditional Japanese mythology continues to inspire filmmakers, modern adaptations have emerged, reshaping these ancient legends into contemporary narratives. The iconic film "Godzilla," whose origins trace back to Japanese monster mythology, stands as a testament to this evolution. In this allegorical tale, the leviathan that is Godzilla represents the wrath of the gods, awakened by mankind's harmful actions. Providing a cautionary tale about the consequences of playing recklessly with nature, "Godzilla" has carved its place in cinematic history, blending ancient myths with modern themes.

Another tribute to Japanese mythology can be found in the film "Kubo and the Two Strings." Drawing inspiration from traditional folktales, director Travis Knight weaves a coming-of-age story that intertwines the lives of mortals and gods. The film's magical landscape reflects the beauty and mystique of Japanese mythology, while exploring themes of destiny, family, and the courage to confront the divine. Through intricate storytelling and breathtaking animation, "Kubo and the Two Strings" represents a heartfelt homage to the ancient gods, and a captivating bridge between tradition and innovation.

Cinema has provided a remarkable platform for honoring the gods and goddesses of Japanese mythology, allowing their timeless stories to transcend centuries and captivate global audiences. Whether through live-action films, animation, or modern adaptations, filmmakers continue to draw from the wellspring of divine inspiration. From Amaterasu's radiance to Susanoo's tempestuous fury, these deities manifest on the silver screen, offering us glimpses of their ancient power and wisdom. As filmmakers continue to pay homage to the Japanese gods, we can only hope that these celestial narratives will endure, reminding us of the eternal allure that mythology holds in our collective imagination.

Contemporary Art: Reimagining Japanese Legends for Today

Art has always been a medium through which artists express their creativity and explore various themes. One such theme that has captivated artists throughout history is mythology and legends. These timeless tales have been passed down from generation to generation, serving as a source of inspiration and fascination for artists worldwide. In this chapter, we delve into the realm of contemporary art, specifically focusing on how Japanese legends have been reimagined and brought to life in the modern era.

Unearthing the Legends:

Japanese mythology is a treasure trove of captivating stories of gods, demons, and supernatural beings. From ancient folklore to literary masterpieces, these mythical tales have shaped the cultural identity of Japan. It is no wonder that contemporary artists have found endless possibilities for reinterpretation and exploration within these legends.

One such artist is Hiroshi Masuda, a renowned painter known for his evocative and dream-like compositions. Masuda frequently draws inspiration from ancient Japanese legends, infusing them with a modern twist. His masterpiece, "The Night Parade of One Hundred Demons," is a prime example of his ability to reimagine and bring a traditional tale to life. In this mesmerizing painting, he portrays a procession of supernatural creatures making their way through a moonlit forest. By employing vivid colors and intricate details, Masuda breathes new life into this age-old legend.

Reimagining with New Mediums:

While paintings have long stood as the primary medium for artistic expression, contemporary artists have constantly sought new ways to reinterpret Japanese legends. With the advent of technology, various mediums such as digital art, installation art, and even virtual reality have become avenues for artists to bring these mythical tales into the modern age.

Take, for instance, the works of Yoko Inoue, a pioneer in the field of digital art. Inoue combines traditional Japanese woodblock prints with modern digital techniques to create visually stunning pieces that reimagine ancient legends. In her series "The Floating World Revisited," Inoue breathes new life into iconic Japanese motifs such as the Great Wave off Kanagawa or the crimson leaves of maple trees in Kyoto. By overlaying digital animations onto these nostalgic images, she transports viewers into a dynamic world where the past intertwines with the present.

Transcending Borders:

Art has always been a universal language, transcending cultural boundaries and connecting people from different backgrounds. This is especially true when it comes to the reinterpretation of Japanese legends in contemporary art. Artists from around the globe, whether of Japanese descent or not, have found themselves enchanted by these mythical tales, leading to the creation of truly diverse and multicultural reimaginations.

One such artist is Lee Mingwei, a Taiwan-born artist known for his thought-provoking installations. In his work "Guillotine in 'The Tale of the Bamboo Cutter," he explores the Japanese legend of Kaguya-hime, a celestial princess sent to Earth inside a bamboo stalk. Mingwei's installation involves a life-size replica of a guillotine blade floating mid-air, symbolizing the impending tragedy of Kaguya-hime's return to her celestial home. Through this powerful and unconventional interpretation, Mingwei pays homage to the timeless nature of Japanese legends while sparking conversations about cultural identity and displacement.

Addressing Contemporary Issues:

Japanese legends not only serve as a source of artistic inspiration but also provide a lens through which contemporary issues can be explored and commented upon. In the hands of skilled artists, these stories can be reimagined to shed light on societal and political concerns that resonate with the modern audience.

One artist who expertly tackles such issues is Tomoko Konoike, a Japanese sculptor known for her fantastical and whimsical creatures. In her installation "The Thousand Arms of Guanyin," she reinterprets the Buddhist deity Guanyin, known for her compassion and ability to extend a thousand arms to aid those in need. However, Konoike's rendition replaces the traditional image of Guanyin with a robot-like creature struggling to balance an array of weaponry. Through this thought-provoking work, she raises questions about the destructive power of technology and the tensions between compassion and aggression in today's world.

Contemporary art has breathed new life into age-old Japanese legends, granting them relevance and relevance in the modern era. From the captivating works of Hiroshi Masuda to the groundbreaking installations of Yoko Inoue, artists have continually sought innovative ways to reimagine these mythical tales. Whether through new mediums, multicultural interpretations, or addressing contemporary issues, these artists have taken the threads of ancient stories and woven them into a tapestry that resonates with audiences worldwide. By constantly reimagining these tales, artists ensure that the legends of Japan remain vibrant, relevant, and everlasting.

CHAPTER 7: THE ETHEREAL CONNECTION

Japan, a country steeped in ancient traditions and timeless beliefs, is known for its rich mythology and spiritual practices that have pervaded every aspect of its daily life. From Shintoism, the indigenous religion of Japan, to the incorporation of Buddhist and Confucian teachings, spirituality is deeply ingrained in the culture, art, and traditions of the Japanese people. In this chapter, we explore the ethereal connection in Japanese mythology and the profound influence it has on spirituality in daily life.

1. The Role of Mythology:

Japanese mythology, derived from a blend of indigenous beliefs and imported philosophies, serves as a foundation for understanding the interconnectedness of the universe and the ethereal beings that inhabit it. Mythology provides a framework for the spiritual practices and rituals that are carried out by individuals and communities alike. It offers explanations for natural phenomena, the creation of the world, and the origin of gods and goddesses.

2. The Shinto-Buddhist Synthesis:

The assimilation of Buddhism into Shintoism played a significant role in shaping Japanese spirituality. During the 6th century, Buddhism arrived in Japan and quickly blended with the existing religious practices. This syncretism resulted in a unique combination of beliefs and rituals, where Shinto deities were incorporated into Buddhist pantheons. The syncretic nature of Japanese religion highlights the adaptability and pluralistic approach of the Japanese towards spirituality.

3. Kami: The Divine Spirits:

Central to Japanese mythology are the kami, divine spirits that are revered and worshipped. Kami are present in various forms, ranging from natural elements like mountains and rivers to ancestral spirits and deities. Shintoism places great importance on the relationship between humans and the kami, emphasizing their accessibility and influence in daily life. Kami are believed to inhabit places, objects, and even activities, creating a profound link between the physical and spiritual realms.

4. Ancestor Worship:

In Japanese mythology, ancestral spirits hold a significant place in the spiritual landscape. The belief in the continued presence and guidance of ancestors is deeply ingrained in Japanese culture.

Ancestor worship involves paying respect to deceased family members, seeking their protection, and maintaining a strong bond between the living and the dead. Ancestor altars, known as butsudan, are commonly found in Japanese homes and serve as a focal point for daily rituals.

5. Rituals and Festivals:

Rituals and festivals play a vital role in connecting the ethereal world with daily life in Japan. Matsuri, or traditional festivals, are celebrated throughout the year to honor specific kami or commemorate historical events. These festivals involve intricate rituals, processions, and performances meant to invoke the presence of the divine and seek blessings for the community. Matsuri are marked by vibrant displays of traditional costumes, music, dance, and food, bringing people together in a shared spiritual experience.

6. Zen Buddhism and Meditation:

Zen Buddhism, with its emphasis on meditation and mindfulness, has had a profound influence on Japanese spirituality. Introduced in the 12th century from China, Zen Buddhism found fertile ground in Japan's cultural landscape. Zen meditation, or zazen, became a popular practice for seekers of spiritual enlightenment. The pursuit of a direct experience of the present moment, known as satori, has guided many individuals towards a deepened understanding of the interconnectedness of all things.

7. Spiritual Reflection in Art:

Japanese art, whether it be painting, calligraphy, or traditional crafts, often reflects the ethereal connection inherent in the culture. The brush strokes of a Zen calligraphy master, the delicately rendered landscapes in ukiyo-e prints, or the intricate details of a tea ceremony are all imbued with a sense of spirituality. These artistic expressions not only demonstrate technical skill but also serve as a means of self-reflection and spiritual exploration.

8. The Way of Tea:

The Japanese tea ceremony, also known as sado or chanoyu, is a ritualistic practice deeply rooted in Zen Buddhism. The ceremony is a symbol of harmony, respect, and purity, reflecting the interconnectedness of the spiritual and physical realms. Participants engage in a highly choreographed series of gestures, involving the preparation and consumption of matcha, powdered green tea. Through the art of tea, individuals strive to cultivate mindfulness and appreciation for the present moment.

Omamori: Protective Amulets and the Kami's Blessing

In the vibrant tapestry of Japanese culture, the spiritual beliefs and practices have left an indelible mark on the country's history. One such tradition that holds a special place in the hearts of the Japanese people is the use of omamori, small protective amulets that serve as a physical embodiment of the kami's blessing. These charming tokens, believed to bring good fortune and ward off evil, have been an integral part of Japanese religious and cultural practices for centuries. This chapter delves into the fascinating world of omamori, exploring their origins, significance, and the rituals surrounding their creation and use.

Origins of Omamori

The word "omamori" traces its roots back to the Japanese language, where "mamoru" means "to protect." Historically, the concept of safeguarding oneself against malevolent spirits or misfortune existed long before the advent of written records. However, it was during the Heian period (794-1185) when Buddhism began to influence Japanese spirituality that the practice of using omamori gained prominence.

Buddhism introduced the idea of charms that carried the power to protect and bring blessings to the faithful. Initially, these protective amulets were exclusively created and used within religious institutions. However, as their popularity grew, they gradually became accessible to the general public. Today, omamori can be found in shrines and temples all across Japan, making them readily available to anyone seeking divine protection.

Understanding the Significance

Omamori hold immense spiritual significance to the Japanese people. They are believed to be imbued with the essence of the kami, the divine spirits revered in Shintoism. These small fabric pouches are made by priests or shrine maidens and are usually stitched closed, leaving only a small opening to allow for the infusion of divine energy.

The amulets are often sewn using brightly colored silk fabric and intricately embroidered with sacred symbols, prayers, or the name of the shrine or temple they originate from. Once complete, the omamori is ritually consecrated, infusing it with spiritual energy and the blessing of the kami. This process enhances the efficacy of the amulet and ensures its supernatural protection for the recipient.

Types and Purposes of Omamori

Omamori are as diverse as the needs of the people who seek them. The most common type is the "tenugui" omamori, a rectangular cloth amulet that can be hung from bags, keychains, or carried inside pockets. These versatile omamori often bear the names of the shrine or temple, as well as an illustration of the deity associated with that particular place of worship.

Specialized omamori cater to specific needs and desires. For instance, "gakugyō-jōju" omamori focuses on providing academic success, while "ekijoji" omamori ensures safe travels. Omamori created to bless marriages, protect against illness, bring prosperity, or provide general good luck can also be found in abundance.

Ceremony and Rituals

The creation and distribution of omamori is a sacred process that adheres to time-honored rituals. Each shrine or temple has its own traditional method, passed down through generations. The production often involves the collaboration of priestesses or volunteers, who meticulously stitch the amulets, invoking divine protection with every precise stitch.

One such example of a ritual associated with omamori is the "Nou-Kata" ceremony, which takes place annually in some Shinto shrines. During this ceremony, the shrine maidens perform a series of intricate dances and sacred chants, while the priests bless and consecrate the amulets with the kami's divine presence. This elaborate ceremony serves to renew the spiritual energy and ensure the ongoing effectiveness of the omamori.

Embracing Omamori in Daily Life

Omamori have become deeply ingrained in the daily lives of the Japanese people. Many individuals carry these amulets with them at all times, treasuring their protective powers and the connection they provide with the divine. Whether it is offering solace during uncertain times, providing a tangible reminder of loved ones, or granting a sense of comfort in the face of adversity, omamori serve as a symbol of hope and faith.

To maintain their potency, omamori need occasional renewal. It is customary to return them to the shrine or temple where they were obtained during the annual Shichi-Go-San festival, a ceremony that celebrates the growth and well-being of children in Japan. During this festival, families visit shrines with their children, offering gratitude for the kami's blessings and renewing the spiritual energy of their omamori.

Shinto Shrines: Daily Visits and the Kami's Presence

Shinto, the indigenous religion of Japan, is deeply ingrained in the daily lives of its people. Rooted in animism and the worship of natural phenomena, Shinto centers around the veneration of kami - the divine spirits that inhabit everything in the world. Shinto shrines play a significant role in the religious practices of Shinto followers, serving as a gateway to connect with the kami and seek their blessings. In this chapter, we delve into the daily visits to Shinto shrines and explore the profound presence of the kami within these sacred spaces.

The Significance of Shinto Shrines

Shinto shrines, known as jinja, hold a vital position in Japanese society. They are not merely places of worship, but also act as community centers, fostering a sense of unity and identity among the people. The architectural design of shrines varies, but they often feature a distinct gateway called a torii, which marks the transition from the mundane to the sacred.

Daily Rituals and Offerings

For many Shinto followers, visiting a shrine is a customary practice that helps establish a spiritual connection with the kami. Daily visits to shrines are quite common in Japan, with individuals seeking solace, guidance, and the blessings of the divine. These visits typically entail a series of rituals and offerings.

Upon entering a shrine, the visitor will cleanse themselves by performing a ritual called temizu. This involves purifying their hands and mouths using a dipper filled with water. This act symbolizes the purification of the body and mind before coming into contact with the divine.

After cleansing, visitors proceed to the haiden, the main hall of the shrine, where they offer prayers and make offerings to the kami. The offerings typically include items such as rice, sake (rice wine), fruits, and flowers. These are placed in front of an altar, with utmost reverence and gratitude for the blessings received.

The Presence of the Kami

It is believed that the kami reside within the sacred spaces of Shinto shrines, making these places a gateway for communication between the human realm and the divine. The presence of the kami is felt throughout the shrine, evoking a sense of awe and reverence in those who enter.

One of the most iconic features of Shinto shrines is the sacred tree, often an ancient and majestic Japanese cedar or cypress. These trees, known as shinboku, are considered the abode of the kami and act as a physical manifestation of their presence. Visitors often find themselves drawn to these trees, feeling a spiritual connection with the divine energy that surrounds them.

The architectural elements of the shrine itself are also designed to enhance the experience of the kami's presence. The main hall, haiden, is filled with symbolic objects, including mirrors, alongside representations of the divine through sculptures and paintings. These visuals serve to remind visitors of the ever-present kami and deepen their spiritual connection.

Perhaps the most profound way in which the kami make their presence known within Shinto shrines is through the phenomenon of yorishiro. Yorishiro refers to objects, often natural in origin, that are believed to act as a vessel or medium for the divine to reside. Common yorishiro include stones, mirrors, and even living animals. These objects are carefully placed within the shrine, allowing the kami to transmit their blessings and power to those who come into contact with them.

Celebrations and Festivals

Shinto shrines are also at the heart of numerous celebrations and festivals throughout the year. These events serve as an opportunity for the community to come together and express their gratitude to the kami. Matsuri, or Shinto festivals, are characterized by lively processions, traditional music, and the performance of sacred rituals.

During these festivities, the kami are honored through offerings of food, music, and dance. The festive atmosphere energizes the shrines, making them an even more potent site for the communion between humans and the divine. These celebrations help to strengthen the bond between the community and the kami, ensuring a harmonious relationship between the human and spiritual realms.

Shinto shrines are not merely physical structures, but rather the rendezvous points where the divine and the human coexist. Daily visits to these sacred spaces provide a means for Shinto followers to connect with the kami, seeking their guidance, protection, and blessings. The presence of the kami is profoundly felt within these shrines, be it through the majestic sacred trees, symbolic objects, or the yorishiro that serve as conduits for their divine energy.

As we have explored in this chapter, Shinto shrines are not only places of religious worship but also central to the cultural and social fabric of Japan. They serve as a testament to the deep-seated spirituality of the Japanese people and the reverence they hold for the natural world. Understanding the significance of these shrines provides insight into the profound relationship between humans and the divine in the realm of Shinto.

Tea Ceremony: A Ritualistic Ode to Harmony and Spirits

In the vast realm of ancient traditions and practices, few have evoked a sense of elegance, tranquility, and spiritual connection quite like the tea ceremony. Timeless in its essence and poetic in its execution, the tea ceremony carries with it a profound symbolism that reaches far beyond the realms of tea-drinking. Originating in the heartland of Japan during the 9th century, this ritualistic ode to harmony and spirits, known as Chanoyu, has become a revered art form, encapsulating centuries of cultural significance and philosophical wisdom. In the following pages, we will embark on a journey to explore the rich tapestry of the tea ceremony, delving deep into its exquisite intricacies, the profound philosophy that underpins it, and the wondrous connection it cultivates between man, nature, and the divine.

The Beginning of the Tea Ceremony

To truly understand the tea ceremony, we must peer into the annals of Japan's history and immerse ourselves in the world of its early practitioners. The origins of the tea ceremony can be traced back to the arrival of tea from China and its integration into Japanese culture during the Tang Dynasty. However, it was not until the 9th century, with the rise of Zen Buddhism in Japan, that the tea ceremony began to take shape as a spiritual practice.

Initially, tea was seen as a medicinal beverage, consumed by monks and nobles in monasteries as a means to achieve states of heightened awareness and mindfulness. These early tea gatherings, known as Chakai, were purely functional, lacking the aesthetic and spiritual depth that would later come to define the tea ceremony. It wasn't until the 15th century that a pivotal figure emerged, altering the course of tea culture forever.

Sen no Rikyū—The Master of the Tea Ceremony

Sen no Rikyū, a tea master of unparalleled skill and insight, was instrumental in transforming the tea ceremony into an art form that encapsulated profound philosophical principles. Known for his exceptional attention to detail and unwavering commitment to simplicity, Rikyū elevated the tea ceremony to a spiritual practice, integrating elements of Zen Buddhism, poetry, and architectural design with the act of tea-making.

Rikyū believed that the tea ceremony should serve as a conduit for connecting individuals deeply to nature, promoting tranquility, and cultivating an unwavering appreciation for the transient beauty of the world. He famously coined the phrase "ichi-go ichi-e," which translates to "one time, one meeting," emphasizing the ephemeral nature of every moment and the uniqueness of each tea gathering. Rikyū's influence was so profound that he effectively established the foundational principles that guide the tea ceremony to this day.

The Tea Room and Its Symbolism

One cannot discuss the tea ceremony without examining the sacred space in which it unfolds—the tea room. Every element within the tea room is meticulously selected to create an atmosphere of utmost harmony and tranquility. From the tatami mats, which evoke a sense of grounding and connection to the earth, to the intricately crafted tea utensils and the tokonoma—a small alcove adorned with a scroll and a carefully chosen piece of art—the tea room is designed as a vessel for spiritual transcendence.

The tea room's humble size serves as a reminder of the intimate nature of the tea ceremony, allowing participants to experience a deep sense of connection to one another and the act of tea-making. The space itself exudes serenity and simplicity, devoid of any unnecessary distractions, inviting all who enter to fully immerse themselves in the present moment.

The Process of the Tea Ceremony

Central to the tea ceremony is the meticulous preparation and serving of matcha, a powdered green tea that signifies the epitome of purity and harmony. The process of making matcha is a carefully choreographed ritual, each movement imbued with meaning and intention.

The host, known as the tea master, meticulously cleans each tea utensil before beginning the process. The teacup, tea scoop, and tea bowl represent harmony, reverence, and purity, respectively. The host expertly measures the tea powder, pouring it into the bowl with precision, before adding hot water and whisking it vigorously with a bamboo whisk until a frothy layer forms on top. Finally, the bowl is presented to guests, who receive it with gratitude and partake in the shared experience of the tea.

Through this ritualistic process, participants are called to focus their attention fully on the here and now, engaging all their senses in the act of tea-drinking. The aroma, the texture, the taste—each element invites the guest to surrender to the present moment, shedding the burdens of the past and the anxieties of the future.

Philosophical Underpinnings

At the heart of the tea ceremony lies a profound philosophy that permeates every aspect of this ancient ritual. Zen Buddhism infuses the tea ceremony, teaching us to find solace in simplicity, to seek perfection in imperfection, and to cultivate a deep respect for nature and the interconnectedness of all things.

Every element of the tea ceremony, from the simple act of cleansing a teacup to the creation of the perfect foam atop the tea, reflects these guiding principles. The tea ceremony teaches us to approach life with humility, to embrace impermanence, and to find beauty in the fleeting moments that make up our existence.

As we draw to the end of this exploration into the tea ceremony, we find ourselves at a juncture where words cannot fully capture the essence of this timeless practice. The tea ceremony, with all its elegance, simplicity, and spiritual depth, defies concise explanation or neatly tied conclusions. It beckons us to engage in its ritualistic dance, allowing us to be consumed by its beauty, tranquility, and the profound connection it fosters between ourselves, nature, and the divine.

To partake in a tea ceremony is to embark on a journey of the soul, to experience a moment of sublime harmony, and to cultivate a deeper understanding of ourselves and the world around us. It is an ode to the impermanent and an invitation to appreciate each passing second with gratitude and reverence. As we bid farewell to the tea ceremony, let us carry its wisdom with us, forever reminding us of the possibilities that lie within the simplest of rituals, and the profound impact that can arise from a humble cup of tea.

Kintsugi: The Golden Repair and Divine Imperfections

In a world often fixated on perfection, where flaws are typically perceived as undesirable, the art of Kintsugi stands as a powerful testament to embracing imperfections and celebrating the beauty in brokenness. Rooted in ancient Japanese tradition, Kintsugi, which means "golden repair," is a delicate art form that boasts a deep philosophical significance. This chapter explores the fascinating world of Kintsugi, delving into its historical roots, technique, and symbolism, and ultimately revealing how it transcends mere craftsmanship to become a powerful metaphor for the human experience.

The Origins of Kintsugi:

To embark on a journey into the art of Kintsugi, we must first rewind time and immerse ourselves in the rich tapestry of Japanese history. The method, though known as Kintsugi, originated during the 15th century, culminating from the Japanese embracing of the ideology of wabi-sabi. Wabi-sabi is a worldview prioritizing the acceptance of transience and imperfections. It finds beauty in the imperfect, the incomplete, and the impermanent – a stark contrast to the Western ideals of perfection and symmetry.

Technique and Process:

Kintsugi is as much a contemplative practice as it is a skilled art form. It involves repairing broken pottery with a specialized adhesive, often a mixture of lacquer and gold or other precious metals. The process is meticulous and time-consuming, requiring not only craftsmanship but also patience and reverence for the broken object.

The first step in the Kintsugi process involves meticulously fitting the broken pieces together, often crafting replacement fragments where necessary. This delicate process demands a deep respect for the pottery's original design and a keen eye for detail. Once the fragments are united, the cracks and gaps are filled with lacquer, creating a stable foundation for the precious metal that will follow.

The final step, often seen as the most transformative, is the application of gold or another coveted metal along the repaired lines. This process is certainly the most visually striking aspect of Kintsugi, as the golden veins trace the history of breakage and serve as a metaphorical reminder of the object's journey from fragility to resilience. The gold-laden cracks transform the pottery's wounds into shimmering scars, turning what was once considered an imperfection into a source of beauty.

Symbolism and Philosophy:

By elevating brokenness to an elevated state, Kintsugi promotes a shift in perspective, urging us to embrace our own flaws and imperfections. Each repaired piece becomes more valuable and unique than its original form, telling a story of survival - a physical manifestation of embracing life's struggles and finding strength within them.

The symbolism of Kintsugi extends beyond the individual object, instilling in us a greater philosophical insight. Just as the ceramic piece is repaired and restored, our own lives follow a similar path. We are all susceptible to fractures, both physical and emotional, but it is through these breaks that we find growth and transformation. Kintsugi becomes a metaphor for the golden repair that occurs within our own lives, reminding us to cherish our scars and appreciate the beauty that emerges from turmoil.

Divine Imperfection:

In the realm of spirituality, Kintsugi also resonates deeply. Many philosophies, particularly in Eastern spiritual traditions, celebrate the concept of divine imperfection – the belief that we are all, in some way, incomplete or flawed. Kintsugi mirrors this spiritual concept by highlighting that the path to enlightenment is not one of perfection but of embracing our imperfections and integrating them into our being.

The art of Kintsugi teaches us that our flaws, just like the broken pottery, are not something to be concealed but rather illuminated. It challenges the notion of perfection and encourages us to recognize that our vulnerability and scars contribute to the richness of our human experience. Through this lens, we begin to understand that the true essence of our being lies not in our perceived flawlessness, but in how we embody our imperfections.

Beyond Pottery: Kintsugi in Everyday Life:

Although Kintsugi originated as an art form for pottery, its principles can be applied to all aspects of our lives. The concept of embracing imperfection and celebrating our cracked nature applies not only to physical objects but to relationships, personal growth, and even societal structures.

As we navigate our way through intricate relationships, we begin to understand that the bonds we forge are often strengthened by overcoming challenges and embracing one another's flaws. The golden repair symbolizes a reconciliation and an acknowledgment that even the most broken connections can be harmonized into something of great beauty and meaning.

On a personal level, Kintsugi prompts reflection on our own journey towards self-improvement. It urges us to view our personal growth not as a quest for perfection but as an evolving process where our cracks and mistakes are embraced, cherished, and transformed into empowering, golden veins of experience.

As we conclude this chapter on Kintsugi and its profound significance, we are left with a newfound appreciation for the art form and the wider message it carries. Kintsugi beautifully exemplifies the human capacity to transform and transcend our hardships, emerging stronger and more resilient. It encourages us to view the cracks in our lives as opportunities for growth and to recognize that imperfections constitute an essential part of our individual and collective beauty.

The art of Kintsugi is a poignant reminder that perfection is not something to be pursued but rather a celebration of the imperfect. It illuminates our path towards self-acceptance, resilience, and ultimately, a profound sense of connectedness. Within the golden repair, we find not only the artistry of a skilled craftsman but also a reflection of our own capacity to mend and transform, turning brokenness into something extraordinary.

CHAPTER 8: CONCLUDING THE DANCE WITH THE KAMI

As we come to the final chapter of our journey through the mystical world of ancient Japan, we find ourselves at a crucial juncture. The dance with the Kami, the revered spirits believed to inhabit the natural world, has been an intricate and profound exploration of the sacred. It has led us through enchanting landscapes, introduced us to captivating legends, and rekindled our connections with the ethereal realm that often eludes our mortal senses. In this concluding chapter, we shall delve deeper into the practices that round off the ceremonial dance, allowing us to bid farewell to the Kami with reverence, gratitude, and hope for continued blessings. Just as the dance began with an invocation of the Kami, it is essential to conclude it with a sense of closure and the understanding that our relationship with these divine beings is ongoing. To conclude the dance with the Kami, one must first reflect on the experiences encountered throughout the journey. Sitting in quiet contemplation, take a moment to recall the sacred sites, the whispers of the wind, and the warmth of the earth beneath your feet. Allow the memories to wash over you, allowing the profound emotions and spiritual connections to resurface. With these memories fresh in your mind, prepare a small altar dedicated to the Kami. This altar should be adorned with natural elements such as flowers, branches, or stones - symbols of the beauty and harmony found in the world around us. Light candles and burn incense, filling the air with fragrant offerings that invite the presence of the Kami.

Next, offer gratitude and respect to the Kami for their continuous guidance and presence in your life. This expression of appreciation should be heartfelt, genuine, and specific, acknowledging individual experiences where the Kami have provided solace, inspiration, or protection. Express gratitude for the lessons learned, the challenges overcome, and the wisdom imparted during the dance.

Following the expression of gratitude, it is time to gently release the connection with the Kami. This is not a severing of the bond but rather an acknowledgment that the dance has reached its conclusion. Take a moment to breathe deeply, visualize the energetic ties that have been formed, and gradually release them into the universe. This act of release allows both the Kami and the practitioner to take what they have learned and experienced back into their respective realms. As the connection eases, conclude the dance with a personalized ritual or prayer. This ritual can be tailored to your own beliefs and preferences, incorporating elements from various spiritual practices or those that resonate most deeply with you. Offer your hopes and dreams for continued guidance, protection, and blessings, both for yourself and for those who dance with the Kami after you.

Once the dance is concluded, take time to reflect on the profound changes and spiritual growth that has occurred throughout the journey. Consider the lessons learned, the moments of personal revelation, and the deepening of your connection with the natural world. In this reflection, you may discover a new sense of purpose, a renewed appreciation for the beauty of life, or a heightened awareness of the interdependence of all beings.

Although this chapter marks the conclusion of the dance with the Kami, it is important to recognize that this is not the end, but rather a beginning. The dance has provided a glimpse into a world where the spiritual and the physical intertwine, where the Kami whisper their wisdom through the rustling of leaves, and where the human spirit can find solace and inspiration. Just as the dance began with an invocation, so too does it conclude with an appreciation for the mystical and the sacred. The connection with the Kami remains open, an ongoing conversation between realms that may be revisited and rekindled throughout one's life. It is a dance that can never truly end, for the Kami are ever-present, waiting to guide and inspire us as we continue to navigate the intricate tapestry of existence.

As the dance with the Kami concludes, remember to carry the lessons learned and the connections made into every aspect of your life. Honor the natural world, seek harmony in your relationships, and cultivate a sense of reverence for the unseen forces that shape our world. By nurturing these practices, we participate in a dance that transcends time and space, allowing the spirit of the Kami to weave its magic into the fabric of our lives.

Legacy of the Kami: Their Everlasting Impact

In the mystical realm of ancient Japan, a divine presence loomed large, shaping the fate of the land and its people. These ethereal beings, known as Kami, were revered as gods and goddesses, bringing blessings and guidance to mortals. The Kami's legacy, an everlasting impact of their existence, can be seen in the religious practices, cultural traditions, and even the collective consciousness of the Japanese people.

The early Japanese society was deeply entrenched in animistic beliefs, attributing spirits to natural phenomena, objects, and even ancestors. This foundation laid the groundwork for the worship of the Kami, and their prevailing influence throughout history. The Kami were associated with various natural elements, such as mountains, rivers, forests, and even celestial bodies. By venerating these entities, people sought favor, protection, and wisdom from the supernatural realm.

One of the most prominent Kami in Japanese mythology is Amaterasu, the Sun Goddess. Believed to be the ancestor of the imperial lineage, Amaterasu embodies the life-giving energy of the sun. Her radiant light brings warmth, vitality, and sustenance to the world. The emperor, as the descendant of Amaterasu, symbolizes the divine connection between the Kami and earthly rulership. Even to this day, the imperial family remains an important and respected institution, perpetuating the Kami's presence.

The legacy of the Kami also manifests in the religious practices of Shinto, Japan's indigenous religion. Shintoism, meaning "way of the gods," places great importance on the worship and reverence of the Kami. Shrines dedicated to specific Kami dot the Japanese landscape, acting as gateways between the human and divine realms. These sacred sites serve as a hub for spiritual and cultural activities, offering solace, purification, and a sense of community.

Throughout the year, festivals known as matsuri are held at Shinto shrines to honor the Kami. These lively celebrations feature vibrant processions, music, dance, and food. People come together, dressed in traditional attire, to pay homage to the deities and express gratitude for their blessings. Matsuri serve as a bridge between the mortal and divine, reinforcing the belief in the ever-present influence of the Kami.

The influence of the Kami extends beyond religious practices and permeates various aspects of Japanese culture. Traditional arts and crafts, such as Noh theater and tea ceremonies, showcase the interplay of human and divine spirits. Noh theater, characterized by its minimalistic aesthetics and profound symbolism, often draws inspiration from mythological stories involving the Kami. Similarly, the tea ceremony, a ritualized practice of preparing and serving tea, embodies the harmony between humans, nature, and Kami.

Japanese literature, too, reflects the imprint of the Kami. Ancient texts like the Kojiki and Nihon Shoki are repositories of mythological tales, documenting the creation of the Japanese archipelago and the divine descent of the imperial lineage. These stories not only preserve the cultural heritage but also reinforce the belief in the Kami's eternal presence.

In Japanese folklore, the Kami continue to be an enduring source of inspiration for artistic expression. Legends about Yokai, supernatural creatures ranging from mischievous spirits to monstrous beings, often feature Kami as central characters. These stories, passed down through generations, entertain and educate listeners about the interplay between humans and divine beings. The legacy of the Kami even extends to the collective consciousness of the Japanese people. The reverence for nature, deep-rooted in Shintoism, has shaped their relationship with the environment. The Kami's association with natural elements and the need to maintain harmony with them has fostered a sense of stewardship of the land. The Japanese people recognize the interconnectedness of all living things and strive to live in harmony with nature, paying homage to the Kami's influence.

Beyond Japan's borders, the impact of the Kami can also be felt in the realm of popular culture. Countless movies, animated films, video games, and manga draw inspiration from Japanese mythology, often featuring Kami as powerful entities central to the storyline. This global fascination signifies the enduring fascination with the divine and supernatural realm in the modern era.

Syncretism: Merging with Buddhism and Other Beliefs

Throughout history, religions have evolved and adapted, often borrowing ideas and practices from one another. This process of merging different belief systems is known as syncretism. In the context of Buddhism, syncretism has played a significant role in its development and spread across various regions of the world. This chapter explores the fascinating phenomenon of syncretism within Buddhism, focusing on how it has assimilated and incorporated elements from other belief systems, along with the historical background and examples of syncretic practices.

A Historical Overview:

To understand the syncretic nature of Buddhism, we must first delve into its origins and early development. Originating in ancient India around the 5th century BCE, Buddhism emerged as a distinct religious tradition due to the teachings of its founder, Siddhartha Gautama, later known as the Buddha. As Buddhism spread outside its birthplace, it encountered numerous indigenous belief systems, resulting in the assimilation of local customs and practices.

1. Syncretism in South Asia:

As Buddhism expanded throughout South Asia, it encountered various religious traditions such as Hinduism, Jainism, and tribal religions. Many philosophical and ritualistic aspects of these indigenous beliefs were incorporated into Buddhism. For example, in areas influenced by Hinduism, deities from the Vedic pantheon were often assimilated into Buddhist worship, granting Buddhism a sense of familiarity to the locals. This blend of traditions ultimately led to the development of unique Buddhist sects and schools.

In northern India, the Buddhist tradition known as the Mahayana emerged, embracing syncretism on a grand scale. Mahayana Buddhism incorporated elements from Vedic rituals, Tantric practices, and even the concept of bodhisattvas, which drew parallels with Hindu deities. The Mahayana tradition also gave rise to the concept of the "celestial Buddha," enabling Buddhists to maintain their devotion to Buddha while also venerating other heavenly beings.

2. Syncretism in East Asia:

As Buddhism journeyed eastward to China, Korea, and Japan, it encountered Confucianism, Taoism, and indigenous folk religions. This encounter led to the development of unique Buddhist schools, such as Pure Land and Zen, which integrated local beliefs and practices into their teachings.

In China, the Mahayana school of Pure Land Buddhism gained popularity due to its syncretic approach. Pure Land Buddhism combined the practice of reciting Buddha's name with the idea of rebirth into a heavenly pure land, akin to the Western concept of paradise. This synthesis of Mahayana Buddhism with indigenous

Chinese beliefs, such as ancestor veneration and belief in celestial realms, struck a chord with the Chinese populace.

On the other hand, Zen Buddhism, which originated in China but flourished in Japan, absorbed elements from Taoism, Confucianism, and indigenous Shinto practices. Zen monasteries became centers of scholastic exchange, artistic expression, and spiritual guidance, fostering a syncretic environment where various beliefs and traditions coexisted harmoniously.

3. Syncretism in Southeast Asia:

In Southeast Asia, Buddhism encountered animistic and Hindu-Buddhist traditions. This interaction resulted in the flourishing of a unique form of Buddhism known as Theravada, which emphasized the path of individual enlightenment. However, Theravada Buddhism in countries like Thailand, Cambodia, and Myanmar often coexisted with animistic practices, belief in spirits, and rituals derived from local folklore. The syncretism seen in Southeast Asian Buddhism illustrates how Buddhism has the capacity to adapt to local religious sensibilities, blending seamlessly with pre-existing cultural and spiritual practices.

Contemporary Examples:

Syncretism in Buddhism is not limited to ancient history. In contemporary times, we can observe how Buddhism assimilates with other ideologies and belief systems in diverse parts of the world. Let's explore a few noteworthy examples:

1. Western Buddhism:

As Buddhism spread to the Western world, it encountered a new set of cultural and philosophical frameworks. Western Buddhists have incorporated ideas from psychology, science, and ecology, integrating them into their understanding and practice of Buddhism. This emergent form of Buddhism is often referred to as "Engaged Buddhism," highlighting the synthesis of traditional Buddhist wisdom with contemporary societal concerns.

2. Buddhism in the Americas:

In the Americas, Buddhism has undergone syncretism with indigenous beliefs. Native American Buddhists often blend their ancestral teachings and rituals with Buddhist practices, creating a unique amalgamation that honors their cultural heritage while embracing Buddhist ideals. This syncretic approach fosters a cross-cultural understanding and promotes harmony between diverse communities.

3. Buddhist-Christian Dialogue:

Another contemporary example of syncretism can be witnessed in the realm of interfaith dialogue between Buddhism and Christianity. Over the past decades, scholars, practitioners, and religious leaders from both traditions have engaged in fruitful dialogue, exploring shared ethical values, mysticism, and contemplative practices. This dialogue has led to the emergence of "Buddho-Christianity" or "Christian-Buddhism," where adherents strive to find common ground, appreciate each other's wisdom, and enrich their spiritual lives.

The phenomenon of syncretism within Buddhism highlights its capacity to absorb, adapt, and evolve over time. By integrating elements from other belief systems, Buddhism has demonstrated its flexibility and ability to resonate with diverse cultural sensibilities. Whether in ancient South Asia, East Asia, Southeast Asia, or in contemporary Western contexts, syncretism has been a significant factor in the expansion and assimilation of Buddhism. This chapter provided an exploration of syncretism in Buddhism, emphasizing historical developments and contemporary examples, showcasing the constant evolution of this ancient tradition through cultural exchange and integration.

www.ingramcontent.com/pod-product-compliance
Lightning Source LLC
Chambersburg PA
CBHW050943050726
47592CB00007B/2415